Connecting the Alphabets

Connecting the Alphabets

Dr Manasi Goswami
Dr Abhilash Nayak

BLACK EAGLE BOOKS
Dublin, USA | Bhubaneswar, India

Black Eagle Books
USA address:
7464 Wisdom Lane
Dublin, OH 43016

India address:
E/312, Trident Galaxy, Kalinga Nagar,
Bhubaneswar-751003, Odisha, India

E-mail: info@blackeaglebooks.org
Website: www.blackeaglebooks.org

First International Edition Published by
Black Eagle Books, 2023

CONNECTING THE ALPHABETS
by Dr **Manasi Goswami** , Dr **Abhilash Nayak**

Cover & Interior Design: Ezy's Publication

ISBN- 978-1-64560-436-5 (Paperback)
Library of Congress Control Number: 2023945055

Printed in the United States of America

Dedicated to
Akshara Brahma Lord Jagannath

Preface

Education is a liberating force. Connecting millions of hearts and souls with an invisible thread, it helps people cut across the barriers of caste, class, creed, gender and religion and fulfill the aspirations in life. Schools being the citadels of education, provide the right environment in which the teachers and students flourish and spread their wings. Putting the welfare of the society and nation over and above their personal interests, teachers groom young minds for a bright future and students follow their dreams under their mentorship. This deep interrelationship between the students and teachers creates wonders. Depiction of the stories of sacrifice, struggle and success of the teachers and students through any written document like a book can boost the morale of good students and teachers, motivate the newly inducted students and teachers to deliver their best and become role models for others.

The present anthology of stories, mostly set in rural scenario of Odisha, India, is a humble attempt to connect the experiences of fourteen characters into an organic whole and present a kaleidoscope of emotions, feelings and thoughts rooted in school life. While trying to teach the learners how to connect or add the alphabets in learning a language, teachers train them to be architects of their own lives, connect the events in their lives and create a successful whole. The events depicted in the stories are a blend of some real life experiences and fictional narratives but the characters very much resemble the people we meet in the schools every day. Each reader will surely find something common with one of these characters and identify himself/herself with them. Most importantly, each story tries to convey a strong message to the society which a sensible reader would never miss. The stories portray and preach a spectrum of qualities that we discover and look for in students and teachers: adaptability, commitment, cooperation, collaboration, enthusiasm, empathy, honesty, intelligence, passion, patience, perseverance, resilience and sacrifice.

It is rightly said that there is divine fire in every human being. One becomes a hero when s/he is inspired and a villain when s/he is tempted. It is the teachers in the schools who know how to ignite this divine fire in their students and channelize their energies in the right direction. The physical infrastructure of an institution is not reflective of its greatness or success. It is the community of teachers who can transform the challenges into opportunities and bring name and fame to the institution. The solutions to all problems lie inside the teachers. Of course, good teachers get incapacitated if the students do not have the urge to grow and surge ahead in life. The success of a school, therefore, solely depends on dedicated teachers who work with their hearts and souls put together and learners who have the drive within them to grow and excel in life under the mentorship of these guardian angels.

Teachers can use this anthology as a Handbook for

Self Development, Learners can use it as a Handbook of Life Skills and the guardians and general public can use it as a Handbook for Guidance and Counseling. Besides dealing with the routine activities of the schools, the book also explores and authenticates the infinite possibilities that lie hidden within human beings, which put to good use can create wonders.

The anthology carries the invisible imprint of the support, cooperation, inputs and sincere wishes of many of our students, friends, colleagues, well-wishers and the technical team responsible for the design and layout of the book. Prof (Dr.) C K Ghosh, Former Director, Regional Services Division (RSD) and National Centre for Innovations in Distance Education(NCIDE), IGNOU, New Delhi, a great thinker, writer and eminent Physicist undertook the responsibility of going through the entire script and gave his invaluable feedback. They all deserve our sincere heartfelt thanks and gratitude for facilitating the publication of this book.

We express our deep indebtedness to Shri Satya Pattnaik, Publisher, Black Eagle, USA and Shri Ashok Parida, Regional Manager of Black Eagle, Bhubaneswar for having taken up the responsibility of bringing out the book in its present form.

We would feel honoured and rewarded if the book gains acceptance among our readers and brings about qualitative changes in their lives.

Ganesh Chaturthi   **Dr Manasi Goswami**

19th September 2023   **Dr Abhilash Nayak**

CONTENTS

Design of Destiny

It was in the year 1980. I was appearing for the matriculation examination. Odashpur High School was the Examination Centre for the students of Kasharda High School. As per the decision of the school administration, all the examinees of our school would stay in a rented house in Odashpur and take the examination under the supervision of two teachers. But my father was not comfortable with this plan as my Aunt's house was in Harirajpur, only two kilometers away from Odashpur. Father went to Aunt's house, checked the distance of the Examination Centre from her house and came back. Finally it was decided that I would stay in Aunt's house and go on a bicycle to take the examinations every day. Being good at studies, I used to stand first in the class. Hence father was of the opinion that if I stayed with other students my studies would be disrupted and I would not be able to prepare well for the examinations. In my Aunts' house I would be under proper care and take the examinations comfortably. Hence accompanied by my father I reached my Aunt's house with my bicycle, books and other belongings. My Aunt's house was in a solitary place. As their children worked outside, only Uncle and Aunt stayed there. Aunt had kept one room cleaned and ready for me. Despite being located in a village, the house was a well-built cement house with big airy windows and facility for a toilet. My Uncle was a retired Auditor. Me and my father went to the school together to get familiar with the road to the school. Father got my bicycle thoroughly checked in a bicycle repair shop so that I did not experience any inconvenience on the days of examinations. Staying for one day in my Aunt's house, father went back to our village. My Uncle was a man of discipline. He checked my pen, pencil, eraser, Admit Card etc. before I proceeded for the examinations every day. He used to wait in the drawing room and audited the question papers when I returned after taking the examinations. He let me go inside the house only after checking the number of questions I had answered right, the questions I had left unanswered and the questions I had answered wrong.

During those days, examinations were being held in two sittings in a day. On the first two days, my performance in the examinations was very good. Especially, Uncle was very much happy and excited for the mathematics paper in which I had answered all the questions right. On that day father had also come on a visit and returned home happy after knowing that I had fared well in mathematics. There was a Sunday in between. The next day was the last day of examination. The examinations of Science and Social Science had been scheduled on this day. As the examinations started at 10 am, I used to start for the Examination Hall at around 8.30 am after having a light rice meal. On that day, Uncle sharpened a couple of pencils, cleaned the eraser and put them in the geometry box as I might require them for making drawings in the science examination. Every day Uncle used to clean the bicycle, put some oil in the chains before I started for the examinations to ensure that I did not have any trouble on my way to the examination. That day too he had kept the bicycle ready for me. I started for the examination after paying obeisance to the home deity, Uncle and Auntie.

After cycling for some time in the low lands, I had to ride up on the highway and then ride on a pitched road up to Odashpur. As it was the main road connecting Kakatpur and Phulnakhra, there was heavy rush of buses and trucks. Usually I reached the school between 9 am to 9.15 am to avoid congestion of traffic. That day too I started in time, crossed the low lands and reached the highway. When I had crossed some distance on the highway, I heard the faint, painful and shrieking voice of a young girl on one side of the road. At first I did not pay any heed to it and moved ahead. I thought since I was going to take the examinations, I should not divert my attention. After pedaling for some time, I could not help my attention getting diverted in that direction. Was there someone lying helplessly? I heard some of her words echoing in my ears and again looked back. Leaning my bicycle against the bush nearby, while putting aside the bushy thickets, what I saw there was staggering. A girl of 9-10 years was lying there in a pool of blood. Her head was fractured and she was bleeding profusely. Painful shrieks came out of her mouth. A basket of flowers was lying upside down at a distance. Perhaps she had been hit when she was plucking flowers from the roadside plants and thrown to this side of the road by a running truck. I was in a dilemma. I could not decide what to do. If I left the girl in that serious condition, she might die. A little of my help, effort and courage might save her life. Haunt by a conflict between my mind and my conscience, I lifted the girl and brought her onto the road. I tried to stop everyone going that way to find out somebody who might know her so that I could take her either to the hospital or to her house with his help and then go to the school to take the examinations. During those days, there was no convention for school boys to wear wrist watches. So I was clueless about the time I had at my disposal and got worried. That place on the road was very lonely. All that I could see there were the express buses which crossed the road by blowing their horns at high pitch. I desperately waved my hands to stop them and ask for help but none of them stopped. After waiting for some time, I lifted the girl and managed to make her sit on the carrier of my bicycle. She was conscious but due to profuse bleeding she did not have enough strength to speak. I used the belt of my school uniform to tie her waist to my bicycle and rolled the bicycle down on the road. On my way, I asked everyone I met to identify the girl and give me a helping hand. But I was not that lucky. None of them could identify the girl and advised me to take her to the hospital and moved ahead.

While coming to Odashpur to check the Examination Centre with my father, I had caught sight of the Community Health Centre. So I hurriedly rolled the bicycle down to the Community Health Centre and reached there. I brought her down from the bicycle, took her inside the hospital and helped her to lie on the bench in the hospital. With my cupped hands, I got water from the nearby tube well and sprinkled water over her face. I used my geometry box to get whatever amount of water I could carry to satiate her thirst. By that time, no one had reached the health centre. Afterwards, a woman reached there with a broom to sweep and wipe the floors. Pointing at the girl, I asked, "Do you know this girl?" She replied in the negative. When asked about the Doctor, she informed me that there was no Doctor in the hospital and only a Compounder managed it. Then she pointed to the Compounder's residence at a distance.

Requesting the lady to have a watch on the girl during my absence, I rushed to the Compounder's residence. When I informed the Compounder about everything in detail, he immediately agreed to come with me. To save time, I brought him to the hospital on my bicycle only. Coming to know about my matriculation examination, he asked me to rush to the Examination Centre and started treatment of the girl. Relieved, I hurried to the Examination Centre in Odashpur High School. I did not see a single examinee on the way to the Examination Centre. I could guess that I had been inordinately delayed. When I reached the school in a state of worry and anxiety, I saw the school gate closed. Worried about my absence, my school teachers Kishore Sir and Prafulla Sir waited for me there at the gate. They asked the peon to open the gate and hurriedly took me to the Examination Hall. By that time more than 15 minutes had elapsed since the distribution of question papers. All my friends were busy writing their answers with their faces down. The Invigilator in the Examination Hall informed me that I could not be allowed to enter the Examination Hall as more than 15 minutes had elapsed since the distribution of question papers. He suggested me that I should go to the Centre Superintendent-cum-Headmaster Shri Braj Kishore Mishra and seek special permission. I rushed to the Centre Superintendent in the company of Prafulla Sir. He could permit if he wanted. When we called on him, he too categorically declined to permit me for being so late. When I showed him my shirt with patches of blood on it and narrated everything, he advised me to understand the importance of time instead of doing social service at such a young age. I entreated him to give me permission "Sir, one year of my life will be wasted" but he turned a deaf ear to my request. Our school teachers also said, "Sir, this boy is one of the best students of our school. His future will be at stake." But the Headmaster was adamant. Ignoring all our appeals, he bluntly declined to permit me to take the examination.

The world before me was full of darkness. Prafulla sir held me in close embrace and brought me out of the school premises. Taking me to a hotel, he offered me a glass of water. We deliberated upon whether I should appear for the second sitting of examination or not. I asked Prafulla Sir to consult my Uncle in this regard. But Prafulla Sir advised me, "Now, you shouldn't waste your time and concentrate on your studies for the next sitting. You can take examination in this paper in the supplementary examination. Let all the examinations be over. Then we shall discuss." My father's face danced before my mind's eyes. I burst into tears out of fear and grief. At that time there was no facility for mobile phones as we have today. So it was not possible for us to send or receive any message. My teachers tried their best to assuage my grief and fear and comfort me. Kishore Sir was a man of short temper. He said, "I had advised your father to permit you to stay with us in the rented house. He did not listen to us. Had he paid heed to us at that time, such an untoward incident would not have occurred." But Prafulla Sir was a man of cool composure. Comforting me he said, "We cannot undo whatever has already happened. You will have to keep your mind cool in such a situation. First of all, you should appear for the last Social Science paper with all attention. Then we shall discuss." I took out the Social Science book from my bag and started reading. I was not able to concentrate but I had no other way out. I went to the Examination Hall in the second sitting. All my friends surrounded me out of curiosity to know why I was absent in the morning session but Prafulla sir cautioned them, "Don't disturb him with your questions now." I went to my seat in the Examination Hall. Sometime after the examinations had started, the Headmaster came panting to our room and looked for me. He came to me, cuddled my head and advised me to do well in the examination. I was amazed to see such a radical transformation in his behavior. He came to our room again when the examination was over and took me to his chamber. He also called my escort teachers from the Kasharda school. I thought that he would either scold me or get my signature on some papers for not appearing the examination in the morning session. But he did not do any of these things. Surprisingly, he sent for the peon to get snacks for us and hugged me. Prafulla Sir and Kishore Sir were also taken aback to see this great transformation in his behavior. The Headmaster said, "You have saved my daughter's life. Had you not taken her to the Community Health Centre in time, she would have lain there unattended and would have lost her life. The Compounder of the Community Health Centre has informed me everything and has taken her to the main hospital in Cuttack in an ambulance for better care and treatment. There are six stitches on her head and she has been kept under observation today. I am also going there now. I am sorry for not having permitted you to take the examination in the morning today. I had never thought that you had made such a noble sacrifice of neglecting your examinations to save the life an unknown girl. Please forgive me." I looked at him in great astonishment. Prafulla Sir came to me and cuddled my head. He said, "At the outset, after noticing stains of blood and soil on his white shirt, I got the impression that he himself had met with an accident. But when Akhil described everything, I was spellbound. I had no words to express my feelings.

Deciding between the question of one's life and that of appearing an examination is no less than an examination itself. And Akhil deserves all appreciation for this." I was pleased to hear what Prafulla Sir said about me. At least he had understood the dilemmatic situation which I had faced. The Headmaster took a piece of *rasgulla*[1] and put it into my mouth. Then he said, "Let us go to Harirajpur, meet his guardians and Uncle and tell them everything."

The Headmaster and Prafulla sir met my uncle and told him everything. My Uncle and Auntie got very worried and panicked. Since I was staying in their home for taking the examinations, they considered themselves guilty for this kind of unpleasant and unfortunate incident. They were both worried and clueless about how to convey this message to my father. By God's grace, that was the last sitting of examination in the schedule. The next day father came to take me back home. After coming to know about my not taking the examination in the science paper, he went silent for some time and then facepalmed. I was very much scared. I could not dare to go near him to pay obeisance to him. My Auntie tried to convince my father. The next day I came home with father with a heavy heart. At first mother was shocked and started weeping when she came to know about the incident. But she was convinced and proud when she knew about the details. While encouraging me to have the resilience to face the situation, she said, "Such selfless service of yours will never go waste. Someone will come to your rescue like an angel when you are in distress."

----

1 *Rasgulla is a popular Indian dessert. The soft round dumplings made from chhena (an Indian cottage cheese) and semolina flour are simmered in a cardamom and rosewater scented
sugar syrup for a tasty sweet.*

Some days after the Headmaster of Odashpur high School came to our home with my Uncle. The issue was thoroughly discussed and it was decided thatI would appear the Science paper in the supplementary examination, pass the matriculation examination, take admission in a college without wasting another year and move on. As matter of fact, this is what exactly happened.

Meanwhile many years have passed. Now I am a highly placed officer in the State Bank of India. My children are pursuing their higher studies. Daughter is pursuing medicine and son has completed M.Tech from NIT Rourkela. My Son Sambit had applied for the post of a Scientist in the Research Centre of Bhaba Atomic Research Centre (BARC), Mumbai and he has been successful in the written examination. Now he has received a letter and email to face the Interview in Mumbai. Till date Sambit has never travelled outside as he has completed his education in Odisha only. So I could not dare to send him alone to Mumbai. I was worried about his travel and accommodation. I had the information that BARC is located in Anushaktinagar, Trombay, in the outskirts of Mumbai. The Interview was scheduled in the month of August. Usually life of people in Mumbai gets miserable during this monsoon season due to torrential rains. Keeping all these things in mind I decided to accompany him and booked two flight tickets and reserved a suite in the State Bank Guest House for two days for our stay in Mumbai. We reached Mumbai one day in advance. BARC was two hours away from the Guest House. Many of the roads in Mumbai had been closed due to incessant rains. The local people suggested that we had to go through a different route, in a roundabout manner. So after having our early breakfast, we started at 7.30 am. We were required to report at BARC at 10.30 am. The interview was scheduled at 11 am.

We could get a taxi easily at the gate of the Guest House itself. The taxi drivers in Mumbai are very gentle and caring. The driver said that we would reach BARC before 10 am. Sambit was busy reading his books for his last-minute preparations for the interview. I was earnestly praying the Almighty for Sambit's success in the interview. Since childhood he had special interest in doing something new and innovative. He would not stop until he finished anything that he was working on. I had the strong belief that his intelligence, working style and perseverance would surely support him in his new job as a scientist. Getting into a job of one's dreams is the first key to success in life. The taxi moved on when I was lost in such thoughts. All of a sudden I noticed that the taxi driver moved the car to the left and stopped it. Before I could say anything, he pressed on his chest tightly and lay down in a half-prostrate position in his seat. He informed us that that he had severe pain in his heart and advised us to take a different vehicle and go. Me and Sambit were perplexed and could not decide what to do. We were scared to see his pain-stricken face. We brought him on to the backseat. Thinking it to be a case of heart-attack, I gave him two tablets of Dispirin, dissolved in water. We were new to the place. We didn't have any clue about the direction in which we were moving, whether there was any hospital in the vicinity or not and the emergency contact number for ambulances in that area. We tried to stop the taxis passing by that road but no one stopped. I told Sambit, "I will take care of the driver. Please take another taxi and go to BARC for the interview." But he did not at all agree to my suggestion of leaving me and the driver in that critical condition. He said, "I had seen a taxi stand on our way to this place. Let me take a snap of this taxi and the taxi driver. I have heard that the Taxi Drivers Association in Mumbai is a strong and systematic organization; they will surely come forward for help when they see the photos and come to know about his situation." Then Sambit took a snap and started running in the opposite direction. I massaged the driver's chest. After a considerable amount of time, Sambit reached there with 2-3 taxi drivers. They called for an ambulance and took the taxi driver to a hospital. I gave them one thousand rupees for the driver's treatment. They were hesitant to take the money but they accepted it after I insisted on it. We hired another taxi and started for the BARC. By that time we had been delayed to a great extent. As it was office time, there was rush of traffic everywhere and it took us more than usual time to travel to BARC. I was very worried and disturbed. Moreover, there are a lot of restrictions in BARC. The taxi driver said that the security staff take snaps of all the visitors at every gate. But Sambit was a man of patience and perseverance. He continued comforting me. By the time we reached the venue, it was already 11 am. All the interviewees who had reported there had been registered. The interview had also started. The Officer in Charge of registration declined to entertain our case though Sambit continued pleading him politely. I too told him about the difficulties we faced on the way. But he said that he was helpless as the computer had turned off the time for registration. He said that Sambit could appear the interview at the end only if the Chairperson of the Interview Board gave special permission. But meeting the Chairperson was almost an impossible task as she was in the Interview Board. Getting her official email ID Sambit wrote an email to her describing all that had happened. But there was no reply. I said, "Let me make a last try as a father and write an email to her from my mail ID. She might reconsider our case after going through the mail." I was shaking in helplessness and could not properly focus on what I was doing. I handed over my mobile to Sambit and he wrote an email from my Email ID informing all the details that had happened. Within two minutes after the mail was sent, a lady came out from the Interview Room and asked the peon near the gate to call Shri Akhil Mohan Sadanagi. We were standing there. We went to her when the peon called us. The lady greeted me and wrote "Permitted" on Sambit's Call Letter and asked him to give it to the Officer at the registration desk. She told Sambit that he would be allowed to face the interview at the end. Sambit was excited and said, "Sure Madam, Thank you Madam. So kind of you." The lady came to me again and greeted me before she entered the Interview Room hurriedly. I breathed a sigh of relief. I prayed and thanked Lord Jagannath in silence. Sambit went to face the interview at the end. Eight candidates who had qualified in the written examination had been called for the interview for only one post of Scientist. His interview lasted for quite a long time. He came out of the Interview Room after nearly one hour. I was scared out of anxiety. I was scared that the Board might have been annoyed for the inordinate delay. After returning from the interview Sambit said, "Yes, at the end of the interview they also asked me the reason for the delay. However, I have been able to answer all the questions of the experts of the Interview Board up to their satisfaction. On the issue of my delay in reporting, the Chairperson appreciated my courage and mercifulness. She said, "Running away from problems should never be the attitude of a scientist."

Other members of the Board also endorsed her views. Let's wait for the results." There was arrangement for lunch for all of us. We came to know that the results would be out in two hours and the successful candidate would be informed through email. After lunch, sitting in the waiting room, we waited for the results. The other seven candidates also waited there in the waiting room. Just at 4.10 pm, the results were notified on the Notice Board. The first person who saw the results came back and congratulated Sambit. I could not believe myself. I asked Sambit to check it himself. When Sambit prostrated before me after seeing the results, I was assured of it. Tears of happiness flowed down from my eyes. Success and achievement of Sambit wiped away all the remorse that I had nurtured amidst the failures and discontentment in my life. Now it was time for us to return. Just at this time a peon came and informed us that the Chairperson wanted to meet us in her chamber. We were worried. Did something go wrong? We followed the peon and entered her chamber. No sooner had we entered her chamber, than she got up from her seat and came towards us. She held my hands in her hands and then paid obeisance to me. I was taken aback at her behaviour. Pointing at the long scar on her forehead she said, "Brother, do you know how I got this scar on my forehead? Do you remember saving the life of an unknown innocent girl 35 years ago? The scar that you see is the result of the injury that I had got in that accident. Yes, I am the same girl, daughter of the then Headmaster, standing before you. I am Dr Anuradha Mishra here, a Senior Scientist and heading the Neutron Physics department. My father always tells me about you. Father got transferred from Odashpur to Capital High School, Bhubaneswar. I studied in Utkal University and

Delhi University and then joined BARC as a Scientist. My father had informed me that you are an officer in State Bank of India. Hence when I came to know about the name, position and State Bank address, I wanted to have a look at Sambit's application. Then I opened his application in my laptop. Sambit has written Kasharda as his permanent address. So I got assured that you are the same Savior of my life."

Anuradha went on speaking, "Sambit has been selected because of his genius and achievements. He has been able to answer the questions of all experts satisfactorily. I have not done anything for him. I have just given him the permission to attend the Interview. My father is still remorseful for not having given you permission on that fateful day. If he comes to know that I have helped you a little, he would have some relief from the self-repentance that he has been going through all these years." Having said this, Anuradha burst into tears. Trying to make her comfortable I said, "No, No, dear, I have forgotten all about that incident. In life we come across many such confusions, dilemmatic situations and problems. We do exactly what our conscience dictates at that particular moment." Then Anuradha asked the peon to get coffee for us and rang up her father. Braj Kishore Sir had retired by that time. Anuradha handed over the phone to me. I could not understand what to say and how to start the conversation. I said, "Sir, I am Mr Akhil Mohan Sadangi from Kasharda. Today by the directions of destiny, your daughter has ensured a bright future for my son." I told him everything in brief. Sir was also pleasantly surprised after knowing about such a nice coincidence. Having offloaded the accumulated grief and self-repentance from his heart, he shed tears of happiness. Such a sweet coincidence enthralled and excited all of us.

Requesting Anuradha to take complete responsibility of Sambit's career, I, along with Sambit started for the Guest House. Anuradha requested us to visit her house but we could not accede to her request. I assured her that we would surely visit her house on the day of Sambit's joining. Sitting in the taxi I reminded Sambit of what my mother often said, "Selfless service will never go waste. Someone will come to your rescue like an angel when you are in distress."

❑

Metamorphosis

After retirement from Jawahar Navodaya Vidyalaya, Munduli in the district of Cuttack as a Music Teacher, I have settled in Bhubaneswar with my husband Satyabrat in my own house. We both spent our entire career in this school. The life style of a teacher in Navodaya is quite disciplined. Getting up early in the morning and joining children in drill, yoga, exercises and sports are mandatory for all. So even after retirement, conditioned by our old habit, we both are used to getting up early in the morning and going out for morning walk every day. While coming back from morning walk, I just can't help buying fresh vegetables being sold along the footpaths. I usually buy green vegetables, spinach, *pudina* (spearmint) leaves, green chilies etc. from the vegetable vendors. As usual that day also I had stooped down and was looking for four good bundles of spinaches from the stack of green leafy vegetables lying before the vendor. Satyabrata had gone a little far. All of a sudden, I heard the clinking sound of a motorcycle parking on the road. Within the twinkling of eyes, a young man in black shirt snatched the golden chain from my neck. One part of the chain remained in my hands as I helplessly grabbed it with one end of my *saree*. The boy ran away from the spot with three parts of the chain.

I was quite lucky. As the boy was driving on the wrong side of the road, the cyclists, motor cyclists and car drivers coming from the opposite side of the road zeroed in on him when they heard my shout "Thief, thief..catch him, catch him." The thief got caught then and there. Having thrashed him black and blue, people took him to the Kharvel Nagar Police Station. Me and my husband had to go to the Police Station to file an FIR. I felt very uncomfortable and guilty. Every day I used to come for morning walk after keeping the golden chain at home but today I came out in a hurry with the chain on my neck. I thought it would have been better if such an unpleasant incident had not taken place.

My husband Satyabrata too used it as an apt opportunity to sermonize me. "Was there any necessity to come out for morning walk with this chain on your neck? Every day you read news about chain-snatching incidents. You could have covered the chain properly with your *saree*." Though I was at fault, I too tried to defend myself with my arguments. This way we both came grumbling to Kharvel Nagar Police Station. The thief was behind the bars. I saw his bearded face, shattered hair and pale countenance. He must be in his twenties. The Officer in Charge gave us the FIR form to fill in. Then he asked me to go near the lock up and identify the boy. I could recognize the boy. He was the same boy who had snatched the chain from my neck. I closely looked at the boy but he did not look up at all. His eyes seemed to be full of remorse. When I went very close to him, he prostrated before me and extended his hands between the bars. Then he tried to touch my feet and wept inconsolably. "Madam, please forgive me." I was taken aback. What is this guy saying? Then I closely observed the boy. He is calling me 'Madam'. Why does he call me so? What does it mean? When my eyes glanced upon the black mole on his nose, I shouted at him, "Are you Ashish?" Then the boy cried with more intensity. Showing the broken chain to him, I asked, "Do you recognize this chain?" Holding both his ears in his hands, he cried. "Madam, I am a thief. I am a criminal. Please kill me with your own hands." Going close to him, I lifted his head from behind the bars and made him sit upright there. Then I took out the water bottle from my bag and splashed some water over his face and wiped it. Asking him to drink two more gulps of water, I said, "Now we cannot undo all that have already happened. Let me see what I can do for you." People who followed me to the Police Station were dumbfounded to see all these. They could not make any head or tail of this development.

Satyabrata too could recognize Ashish. We both approached the Police Officer and told him that we wanted to withdraw the FIR. As the culprit was our student, we both appealed the Police Officer to spare him. But the public who had nabbed him protested, "If we let the boy go scot free like this, he would get the courage to repeat such crimes in future. It is true that he is known to you but by now he must have done a lot of damage to many unknown people and will also do so in future."

The Officer in Charge was also hesitant. He said, "Even if you don't file an FIR against him, the police will have to file an FIR on its own. The stolen item has also been seized from him and he has also confessed to the crime of snatching your golden chain. Moreover, the public have brought him here. Sorry Madam, we are bound to file the FIR. Today he will be inside the lock up and tomorrow he will be forwarded to the court." Me and Satyabrata felt helpless. I felt guilty. My eyes welled up with tears. The police put together the broken parts of the chain left with me and the part which Ashish had snatched and sealed them in a box. Then the Officer in Charge said, "We will return it to you once the matter is settled in the court of law."

With the permission of the police I gave Ashish some biscuits, fruits and a bottle of water and returned home with a distressed and dilemmatic mind. I did not feel like doing anything that day: neither cooking, nor eating, nothing. The whole day I felt repentant as it was because of me the poor fellow was behind the bars.

After fifteen days, I got a call from the Police Station. Ashish's trial was carried out through fast track. He had been sentenced with three months' imprisonment as he was a juvenile. He had been sent to Jharpada Jail for three months. The Officer in Charge returned my chain in a sealed box. With a heavy heart, I returned home with the chain. I could not even get a chance to meet Ashish. I did not feel like opening the box to see the chain. I kept the chain in the Almirah and wept to my heart's content.

Two months had elapsed meanwhile. I intermittently enquired of the Officer in Charge regarding Ashish's whereabouts. Having contacted the Jailor, he informed me that he was doing fine. As Ashish was a well-behaved and hard-working person, there should not be any problem for him to get released early.

Today was the 26th of June. According to the Jailor, Ashish's papers would be kept ready by 11.30 am and he would be released. I informed Satyabrata, hired a familiar auto rickshaw and went to the front side of Jharpada Jail. I waited for Ashish in the auto-rickshaw. At around 11.45 am, Ashish came out of the main gate of the jail with a bag in his hand. I rushed to him. Ashish hugged me and wept miserably. I offered him a bottle of cold drink. He drank it and felt comfortable. Dragging him to the auto, I said, "Ashish, let us go home. You will stay with us for some days and then you can go." He was hesitant but I did not let him have his own way.

On our way home, I got the auto parked near a saloon and got his hair and beard done. When he was inside the saloon, I got him a pair of banyans and barmudas. Then we both got home in the same auto. Satyabrat was a little surprised to see Ashish with me. I said, "He has no one to call his own. I am planning to keep him under our care in our house for some days, make him mentally healthy and then let him go." As Satyabrata too was his teacher, he could not decline my suggestion.

There were two garage rooms in our house. Satyabrata had constructed them in case our son got transferred from Delhi to Bhubaneswar and he would require a garage for his car. One of the garages was lying unused. I provided a charpoy, a fan to Ashish and made arrangements for his stay there. After a long time, Ashish had a proper bath and put on the new clothes. He looked a little fresh and healthy. As it was a hot summer day, I treated him with curd rice and potato *badi chura*[2] and he had bellyful of it. I felt very happy and contented. I told him, "First of all, you should have some good sleep. Then we will discuss."

Ashish had a sound sleep until evening. As if he had got a mother's love-laden lap after so many days. As usual, I offered evening prayers before the *Tulsi* (basil) plant,

---

2 *Badi chura: A coarse crushed mixture of sun-dried lentil dumplings (Badi), onion, garlic, green chilies and mustard oil, used as a delicious item with the Odia cuisine*

prepared a cup of tea and called Ashish. Out of joy and excitement, Ashish gulped the tea and said, "Madam, please sit beside me and cuddle my head with your affectionate hands. After so many days I have been able to listen to your affectionate call 'Ashish'. Madam, I feel as if I have taken rebirth." Meanwhile Satyabrata too joined us, seated himself on Ashish's bed with the cup of tea in his hand.

Then Ashish continued, "Madam, I had recognized you when I was trying to snatch away your necklace and you looked back at me while trying to grab your saree with your hands. After looking at the broken chain in my hands, I too could identify the chain.

Sandwiched between deep anxiety and dilemma, I got absentminded and could not focus on driving my motorcycle properly. Hence people could easily catch hold of me and pounced upon me. In fact, after being nabbed by people I was very happy. I thought that at least it would give me a chance to beg your forgiveness. I would be able to wash your feet with my tears of remorse."

I said, "Yes Ashish, this is a chain with magical powers. I very much remember the Annual Function of Munduli School. As the music teacher, I had the responsibility of organizing the cultural programme. And you were my right hand. You were an expert in playing the *tabla*. You always volunteered to help me in everything, be it the morning prayer or any cultural programme of the school. You used to supervise the maintenance and transportation of the musical instruments. The rehearsal of the cultural program was in progress on the eve of the Annual Function. You were playing the *tabla* in harmony with the tunes of my harmonium. All of a sudden, I discovered that my golden chain was missing. I got very worried and disturbed. The chain was brand new. It was of a different design, a double-layered gold chain with pea-like beads. Me and Satyabrata, your Sir had purchased it from Cuttack a few days ago with a lot of enthusiasm. I was greatly disturbed as I had lost the chain. You searched for the chain everywhere on the stage. A few of your friends too joined you in the search for the chain in the nearby areas. All the classrooms which I had visited that day were thoroughly searched but all was in vain. The chain was not to be seen anywhere. It seemed as if it had miraculously vanished.

The next day was the Annual Function. I came early in the morning and again l thoroughly looked for the chain everywhere, under the stage, on the stage, on the staircase, under the staircase, garden, back side of the stone statue but without any success. I was very disheartened. Your Sir too got worried. He said, "It was a heavy chain of 20 grams. How come that you couldn't notice when it fell off your neck?" It is also believed that losing gold is not auspicious. My mind was tired and gloomy. However, hiding all the pain and sadness in my heart, I could successfully conduct the cultural program on that day. The senior officers of Navodaya Vidyalaya Samiti had come from Bhopal. The art and culture of Odisha, particularly the classical Odishi dance enamored them and they were full of appreciation. But lost in the sadness of losing the chain, my heart could not relish their appreciation and was grieving in agony time and again."

Interrupting me Ashish said, "Madam, let me narrate my part of the story". Addressing Satyabrata he continued, "Yes Sir, Madam's face had turned pale. So I too did not feel comfortable. Children got two days of holidays after the Annual Function. All were happy. But my eyes were looking for Madam's chain everywhere. The chain danced before my mind's eyes. Without the chain, Madam looked graceless and gloomy. Every day I looked for the chain for one to two hours. This way five days elapsed in between. Gradually my hope of getting the chain back got faded out. On the sixth day, for reasons unknown to me, I came to school with a stick. The school gardener had arranged bougainvillea flowers in big cement pots. I thought of checking all the cement pots carefully. At the same time, I was scared that the gardener might scold me if any of the pots got damaged. Therefore I reached near the stage before the gardener came. I didn't get anything in the first three pots. The fourth one was full of yellow flowers. There were thorns on the branches. It was a big old plant. Hence I put aside the flowers, leaves and thorns with the stick. Suddenly I found the dazzling chain hanging from the thorn on one branch of the plant and playing hide and seek in the faint beam of light coming from the main gate. With a lot of care, I took Madam's chain from out of the thorns, held it close to my heart and ran towards your residence. Madam, I cannot express the joy and happiness I experienced at that moment. I went on banging the door and shouted 'Madam, Madam' without bothering to press the calling bell. After opening the door, you both were overjoyed to see the golden chain in my hands. You hugged me and Sir patted me on my back. Oh Madam, I felt as if I had bagged a gold medal in the Olympics."

We all went silent for some time. Then I asked Ashish, "The same year me and Sir got superannuated from Munduli school. At that time, you were in Class X. Under what circumstances have you landed up in this world of crime?" Ashish kept quiet for some time with his face down. Then he narrated, "Madam, I got promoted in Class X. Then I got admitted in the Science stream for higher secondary studies. There was no Arts stream in that school but my mind was inclined towards Arts subjects. After your retirement, no music teacher joined that school. So there was no scope for practicing song or music. I could not understand the science subjects properly. In the +2 Science stream, the students and the teachers focus on studies, entrance examinations, board examinations etc. But science was not my cup of tea. I did not like the science subjects at all. Meanwhile another incident took place. One day I had planned to see the Khandagiri festival with a friend from Munduli. When I was trying to jump over the boundary wall in the night, I was caught red-handed by the Headmaster. He troubled me a lot, called my father and sent me home for a week. My journey to home was destined to be a journey of no-return. My father and uncle tried to persuade me to go back to the school and continue my studies but in vain. Having been annoyed and disgusted with the grumble and taunt of my father, one day I fled from home and came running to Bhubaneswar. The boy from Munduli trapped me in this dirty business. I have been doing this heinous work for the last two years."

There was pin drop silence for some time. Breaking the silence I said, "We have no control over whatever happened as it was destined to happen. That has become a thing of the past. Now it is time for us to decide upon the future course of action. There is no question of your going back to that world of crime. Now you should think of earning your livelihood by doing some good deeds." With a cool and balanced mind I put forth a proposal, "We both have become lonely and helpless after retirement. Both our son and daughter-in-law are settled in Delhi. This house looks secluded and lonely. After a busy and hectic life in Navodaya Vidyalayas, it has become very difficult for us to live a monotonous life like this. This never-ending retired life has become very boring and painful. My love for music has also got subdued. Without proper care, the musical instruments are lying unused and gathering dust. How about Ashish and me starting a music school for the small children of the colony in this garage? Moreover, the house would buzz with the *bhajans*, prayers, classical songs and notes. Of course, the income from this may be meager but Ashish can live comfortably with us." Excited at the proposal, Satyabrata said, "Wonderful idea! Everyone's life would resonate with this new innings. Hello Ashish, can you start a new life by creating a new harmony on the harmonium and *tabla* under the mentorship of your Madam? Moreover, you can also continue your studies through distance mode from NIOS and IGNOU, rise in life and chase your dreams."

Out of love, respect and happiness, Ashish got down from the charpoy, held our feet together tightly and said with a note of gratitude, "You have shown me a new way of life. My soul would get a new lease with song and music." Overjoyed, we all hugged one another.

The next day Ashish went to the goldsmith's place, got my chain repaired and put it round my neck himself. After a week "The Sai Ashish Music Centre' got launched in our garage.

❑

A Handful of Alphabets

During recess we all ladies teachers were engrossed in delightful chitchatting over lunch in the Teachers' Common Room. It was the Mothers' Day. The eyes of teachers were glued to their mobile screens. Their children staying outside were wishing them 'Happy Mothers' Day'. Mothers were happy by reading the WhatsApp messages and emails. Just at this time peon Radha came inside the Teachers' Common Room and told me, "Madam, there is a letter for you. The postman wants you to sign and receive it." I got up in a hurry and went out. After receiving the letter, I entered the staff common with a smile. All present there looked at me. I had been transferred to the school just one month ago. Hence my lady colleagues were not very much familiar with me. Tarulata Madam asked me, "Meenakshi, Do you still resort to the practice of writing letters for communication with dear and near ones? We communicate through WhatsApp and emails only." I said in reply, "Yes, I too have WhatsApp and Email accounts of my own but I prefer to exchange letters with a few selected people on special days."

I opened the letter with a lot of excitement. It was a beautiful envelope. Inside it there was a letter as well as a poem written on a colourful and artistically designed sheet of paper. Kalyani Madam asked me, "Oh! What a beautiful letter! So nice Odia letters! Who has written it?" I cheerfully replied, "My son Teertha. He has sent me a poem and a letter to wish me Mothers' Day." "Oh Great!! A poem for Mother on the Mothers' Day! Meenakhi, Please read it out. Let all of us listen to it. We are not lucky enough to receive handwritten letters from our children." Kalyani Madam said. I read out the poem:

Gulping the poison of all sorrows and pains
Like a Neelakantha,
You can give away nectar of love to all;
Dying a hundred times everyday
You can beg for a hundred year's life for me.(1)

From the lava of the volcanoes
You can create a mountain of cool affections;
Wiping out my tears with your words of comfort
You can build a castle of dreams for me. (2)

Let my soul never be stained with
My futile efforts to find alternatives to your love
The futile arrogance of paying back your debts;
I flourish in the garden of your love and self-esteem
In the garden of my life
Let your motherhood spread its fragrance like
The fresh blossoms for me. (3)

By the time I completed reading the poem, my throat got choked. All teachers were looking at me with attention. Having said, "Wonderful!" Anuradha Madam patted me on my back. She asked me about Teertha. I said, "He is now studying in IIM, Kolkota. He has a hobby of writing poems in Odia and English. He has also got training in Odishi classical music. So, he also sings classical songs. Since his childhood I have tried a lot to make his handwriting beautiful. Often I have hit his little fingers. I used to give him small stories and poems to copy to practice good handwriting. So while learning good handwriting, he also started enjoying the beauty of stories and poems. In spite of the regular communications that we carry out through WhatsApp and emails, we make it a point to communicate through handwritten letters on important days. Dear Madam, I don't know how long I can continue with this practice in this hectic life." Having said this, I carefully kept the letter in my bag.

At this time, Radha came again and called from the door, "Pratima Madam." Pratima Madam said, "Are you saying something to me?" She replied in the affirmative and showed a blue Inland Letter. Pratima Madam went out to the verandah. Coming back after some time, she said, 'It's a letter from Radha's son. She cannot read the letters. So whenever there is a letter every week, she calls me and asks me to read it out for her. His son's handwriting is so bad and the syntax is so faulty that I find it very difficult to understand them and explain their meaning to Radha. I think his son is educated up to Class IVth/Vth. He has got a vegetable shop in Cuttack. But every week he at least remembers to write a letter to his mother. As Radha cannot use the mobile, her son always writes letters to her regularly to keep her informed about his whereabouts."

After a few minutes' silence, Pratima Madam looked at me and said, "Do you know Meenakhi, I get into a melancholic mood after reading the letters of Radha's son. At least her son remembers to write letters to his mother expressing his thoughts; it doesn't matter whether the handwriting is bad or the sentences are faulty. But my son just manages with a video call of 2 minutes at a gap of two weeks. He thinks that he is done with his responsibility. He remains so busy that we do not even dare to make him calls, in case his work might be affected. When I see Radha tying the letter in the end of her *saree* and tucking it in her waistline, I think she is much more fortunate than me."

Interrupting her, Minati Madam said, "Pratima, really the experience of receiving and reading handwritten letters is something very unique. Receiving a handful of alphabets from our own children whom we taught the alphabets has become almost a distant dream for us. Children are away from us, earning a lot of money. Their jobs in the MNCs have deprived us of the reality of the uniqueness of our lives. We are forced to live lonely for years just by consoling ourselves with the video calls with our children." Minati Madam heaved a deep sigh. Padmaja Madam picked up the discussion, "Yes, that's right. Emotions have become unrealistic. Children often keep us comforting that we should be progressive and adaptive to the emerging needs of time. On our marriage anniversary, our son from Australia ordered for a big cake from a local shop and got it sent to us. Looking at the cake I could not control myself. Everything looked to me out of context, unrealistic and snobbish. Had I received a hand-written letter in place of all these, I would have read it five times and held close to my bosom 10 times and would have kept it under my pillow for at least a month. Padmaja Madam could not continue as her eyes had got welled up with tears.

I was a little disturbed to notice this kind of agony, anguish and lamentations of motherly souls on such a memorable day. I had never thought that a poem from Teertha and a letter from Radha's son would create so much of turbulence and emptiness in their hearts. Mothers' souls are always contented with 'little' things. They get enthralled when their children first address them as 'Mother'. Now children have discovered easy and handy alternatives to the 'little' that the mothers want and have started using absurd symbolic messages and SMSs. I was very perturbed. I thought "Have we turned into machine-run robots, bereft of any sensitivity and feelings? In our generation, we still have some sensitive souls and hearts around us. But what about the next generation? They may not have anyone to consider them their own, sympathize with them and stand by them in their time of need. Can the social media like WhatsApp, Twitter and Facebook provide support to them in their life filled with emptiness? A mother has to go through so much of struggle during the life-cycle of a human being, right from lifting a child from the ground to transforming him/her into a social being. It's the mother who pioneers in teaching the Book of Alphabets, handwriting and all kinds of knowledge like literature, mathematics and moral education to their children. It's none but a mother who provides courage to the child to continue his/ her studies in the teeth of sorrows, poverty, disease, defeat and agony. But now the modern children have learnt the language of computers and have completely forgotten their mother tongue. Can anyone progress in life and understand the language of computers without learning the mother tongue?

My heart got heavy with all such thoughts. I thought If Teertha too goes to a foreign country for employment and forgets his Odia and Odishi music, won't my motherly soul be troubled? I came home with all these never-ending thoughts. But I made up my mind to do something about it.

Within two -three months I could easily collect the email IDs and WhatsApp numbers of the sons and daughters of my colleagues without the knowledge of their mothers. Many of them were well-settled in good positions in India and abroad. Some of them are in India whereas some others are in Odisha. Many of them are also married. One day I wrote a well-thought-out interesting letter to all these children. I tried to convey to them the crystal-clear thoughts and expectations of their mothers. The pleasure obtained from employment and power is not sufficient to make their life easy and elegant. Social and family relations have a different power and impact of their own. A mother's inspiration is the strongest motivational force for a person. This power makes the inaccessible accessible and the impossible possible. So, if you can understand the mind of your mother, no wisdom of the world will remain inaccessible and incomprehensible. Having put down my thoughts in this elegant and convincing style, I sent an email to all of them. But after sending the emails I wondered whether the children in such high positions would accord any importance to the email of an ordinary school teacher.

After a couple of weeks, replies started flowing in. My heart-touching letter had left a deep impression on all of them. They had respected my innovative initiative with gratitude and thankfulness. I was in touch with all the 24 children of my 17 female colleagues at regular intervals and had cautioned them to maintain secrecy about our communication and not to inform their mothers about this.

Time rolled on. I wrote another letter to all children

two months before the Mothers' Day. I suggested that they should plan to do something on this Mother's Day to give a pleasant surprise to their mothers. Each one of them would write or draw something interesting and send them to their mothers at their school address. They would not use WhatsApp, SMS or email to wish their mothers either on the same day or before the Mothers' Day. They could write poems, stories or draw pictures as per their choice and send them to their mothers in such a way that they would reach the post office either one or two days before or on the Mothers' Day. I would request the Postmaster and the postman to deliver the letters to the recipients on the Mothers' Day only.

Children also found it interesting to engage themselves in such an exciting game with their mothers after a long gap. Some of them emailed to me, "Auntie, my Odia handwriting is so bad that my mother cannot read them." I wrote back to them with the reply, "When you were an infant, your mother understood whatever you said through your broken language. Will it be difficult for her to understand your letter written in badly shaped letters? "You make a try. Mothers can understand everything. Having maintained communication with them in this manner, I inspired them to present their mothers with a unique and pleasant gift on the Mothers' Day.

Mothers' Day arrived very soon. We were all busy in taking our classes in the school. All the teachers came to the Teachers' Common Room during recess. They were all worried and curious as none of them had received any phone call or message from their children since the morning. They assumed that being busy with their hectic work schedule, their children had even forgotten to send a message. But no one asked anyone about it. The only thing they discussed was that there was no proper mobile network in the school. A couple of them went outside and checked their mobile networks. Sitting in a corner, I observed everyone. All the teachers seemed to be very uncomfortable. But no one expressed their discomfort of not getting the Mothers' Day message before others.

Just at this time Radha came and called, "Madam, please come, sign and take your letter." No one got up. I got up and went outside. While coming to the school I had requested the Postmaster to send all the letters to the school at 1 pm. Coincidentally, the postman Murali was the father of one of our alumni. So, he cooperated with me in this matter. He had come with all the letters that had come before and the letters that had reached that day. Coming outside, I again sent Radha inside. I said to her, "Radha, go and call all the teachers. All have got letters and they will have to sign to receive them." All the teachers were dumbfounded when they reached the postman. Everyone had one or two letters in big envelopes. First of all, I received my letter and got back to the staff common room. Asking Radha to bring us hot tea and *samosas*, I waited for the other teachers to return to the Teachers' Common Room. Coming back, they all started opening the envelopes curiously. Sitting in a corner, I took snaps of these scenes and all were unaware of it. I did so as it was my responsibility to send the snaps of these unique scenes to their children. The daughter of one of the teachers had sent a self-painted beautiful oil painting of her mother. The son of another teacher had sent a list of the food items that his mother used to prepare in his childhood days. This was accompanied by a nice song. Almost all the children had sent poems, letters, stories, cartoons, drawings, posters, depicting the pleasant and memorable experiences related to their mothers. The lonely Teachers' Common Room, filled with the pristine happiness oozing out of the mothers' hearts, looked like a divine garden. Seeing my colleagues experiencing motherly happiness and excitement, I experienced a unique ecstatic joy. At last, I was successful in my endeavour and my efforts put in for one year had given results. After the session of letter reading was over, everyone wondered how this could happen. After such a long time, how could their children send hand-written letters, paintings, poems, cartoons on the same day? Did they all do this on their own? Their glances and doubts were fixed upon me as I was sitting in a corner and taking their snaps and video recording them. Padmaja Madam came and hugged me. She said, "Meenakhi, I am sure that you are at the root of this heart-touching programme. No one other than you can think so creatively and meticulously. How could you bring all our children together and plant such wonderful ideas into their minds?" I smiled and said, "Madam, our children love their parents very much. But the modern e-gadgets have changed the mode of expressing their love for their parents. We will have to revive that old tradition. While learning how to do things with the minimum effort, with utmost 'economy', they have also used the same 'economy' while expressing their love and affection. Hence we need to write hand-written letters to them so that they will get used to them. We too have to make our own efforts in this regard."

Anuradha Madam said, "Now, let's listen to your son's poem. I said, this year Teertha has not sent me a poem. He has sent me the YouTube Link containing the popular 'Ma' song in his own voice. I played the song for them on my mobile. The song came from Teertha's melodious voice.

My mother
Greater than the sky, deeper than the ocean
The best and sweetest name
That people in the world reckon.

They all got emotional while enjoying the song. The valedictory moments of Mother's Day with hot tea and Samosas were very much enjoyable and memorable.

❑

Award within an Award

Shrihari Sir raised the issue over a cup of tea in the Teachers' Common Room. The Headmaster was busy in writing something with his face down. The other teachers were also busy in sipping tea. All of a sudden everyone looked up at Srihari Sir when he said, "Our colleague Binay's reputation has spread far and wide. He has earned a lot of fame by attending conferences, meetings and writing books. He has also contributed a lot to community development and promotion of sustainable lifestyle among the people in the area. It is because of his hard work and commitment that the students of our school have also figured in the top ten list of the board examination. In my opinion, he should apply for the President's Award for Teachers this year. We would have been happy if our school could get an award like this before we all old teachers retired. What do you think Ramakrishna Babu?"

Having said all these things in one breath, Shrihari Sir looked at the Headmaster.

The Headmaster Ramakrishna Sir also got encouraged at such a nice proposal. Sipping tea from the cup he said, "Definitely. There cannot be a second opinion about it. Mr. Binay, please go tothe BEO Office urgently, get a form and apply for it." Ratnakar Sir, sitting close to him, added, "Mr Binay, let the President's Award for Teachers come to Narendranath Vidyapeeth this year."

Binay Sir, the Science TGT of the school, was seated in a small chair in a corner of the room. He was bewildered to suddenly overhear such a discussion about him. In his usual tone of humility he said, "No Sir. I don't consider myself suitable for such a great award. That you all consider me suitable for such a prestigious award is itself an award for me." Interrupting him, Ramakrishna Sir said, "Nothing doing. Please go to the BEO Office tomorrow itself and bring the application form. Even today teachers enjoy a dignified position in this country. Your efforts, initiatives and achievements in teaching and learning will be surely evaluated and rewarded."

Being a young and junior teacher, Binay Sir could not say anything in the face of the Headmaster. Till date he has not even dared to have a cup of tea in front of him. He considers Ramakrisha Sir a fatherly figure and has a lot of respect for him. So he preferred to keep quiet.

It is because of Ramakrishna Sir that it has been possible for Binay to grow up professionally as a teacher. All these seem to have happened within a span of few years only. Binay's father succumbed to death when a thunderstorm struck him when he was working in the fields. So his mother had to leave home to work outside to manage the family. This put an abrupt end to Binay and his elder brother's education. At that time Binay might be either in Class III or Class IV. Binay's mother could just manage to make both ends meet for one year with much difficulty. Later on, she got work as the cook for the midday meals in the school. Every day, while coming to the school, she brought Binay along with her to assist her in cooking. Binay had been forced by his circumstances to leave school but he had not given up his interest for studies. So he loved to accompany his mother to school for assistance in cooking, even though it was not for studies. After having helped his mother, he often sat in the classrooms with other children. Class V was the room next to the kitchen. The dividing wall was made up of palm leaves and tree trunks. Hence he could clearly and carefully listen to whatever the teachers taught in the next room. He used to borrow books from children during recess and read them at his convenience. One day Ramakrishna Sir was teaching science in Class V. He said, "Children, I taught 'Lever' in the last class. Could you give me an example of a class three lever? There was utter silence in the class. They all wondered what could be a class three lever. They got engrossed in this thought and went silent. Observing the silence of children for such a long time, Binay could not control himself. He snatched the pliers from his mother, pushed it through the gap in the wall of trunks and said "Sir, this is a class three lever." Children could not help laughing when they saw the pliers projecting out through the gap of the trunks. They all fell silent when Ramakrishna Sir reprimanded them. Ramakrishna Sir was both delighted and amazed to see such intelligence and presence of mind in Binay who could cite such a live example. Then he called Binay to the class and asked him some more questions related to his subject. He was very happy to see the way Binay faultlessly answered the questions. Noticing such an ardent desire for studies in the child, Ramakrishna Sir decided to educate Binay. He thought that the creativity, skills and intelligence of the boy should not go waste. At that time Mr Madan Mohan Panigrahi was the Headmaster of the school. Ramakrishna Sir got Binay admitted in Class

V after due consultation with the Headmaster and bore all the expenses for his studies.

Binay had a lot of commitment and interest for studies. So Ramakrishna Sir did not hesitate to spend on his education. Binay had a very simple life style. In order to save paper, he used a slate and chalks to do all rough and numerical works until he completed Class VII. Being first in the district, he got scholarship in the board examinations in Class V and Class VII. Biany's success was a challengeable goal for Ramakrishna Sir. In spite of being a low-salaried school teacher, he selflessly went on supporting Binay for his education. In course of time Binay passed the matriculation examination in first division with good percentage of marks. Now it was time for Binay to study in a college! At that time, Ramakrishna Sir's elder son was studying in college and the younger one was in school. So there was need of money. But for someone hell bent upon creating good human beings, money could not be an impediment. Ramakrishna Sir was an expert in writing articles and making inexpensive science equipment. No one could equal him in teaching science. Hence he took keen interest in writing books and preparing science projects and equipment. He used most of his spare time in writing books for children, explaining the difficult concepts of science in books for science teachers, preparing science teaching models, science toys using waste materials. Such books and Teaching Learning Materials (TLM) for science were very useful for the practicing teachers as well as the teacher trainees. Though the income from publication of books and sale of Teaching Learning Materials was not very encouraging, it was a great financial support to him during that critical time.

With the support of scholarship, tuitions and financial assistance from Ramakrishna Sir, Binay successfully completed BSc. He too aimed to be a competent and popular teacher like his role model Ramakrishna Sir in his life. So he did not take interest in any other job and opted for training for B.Ed. at Regional Institute of Education(RIE), Bhubaneswar. He was the topper among the first division holders in the B.Ed. Examination. Meanwhile Ramakrishna Sir took over as the Headmaster of Narendranath Vidyapeeth. There were many posts of teachers lying vacant in the school. So when Binay was successful in the teacher recruitment process, Ramakrishna Sir requested the Circle Inspector to appoint him in his school. As the school was located in a Sub-Division, there was no pressure from any other teachers showing interest to come to this school. Therefore, Binay could easily get appointment in this school. Having paid his obeisance to Ramakrishna Sir, student Binay started his teaching career as Binay Sir, the teacher Binay. Ramakrishna Sir didn't maintain any official formality while addressing Binay in the school and addressed him informally. Binay put in all sincere efforts to become a competent science teacher like Ramakrishna Sir. Just like Ramakrishna Sir he too involved himself in preparing Teaching Learning Materials for science, writing books on different teaching methods, science and popular science fiction with a lot of interest and commitment. When the aim is noble and there is sincerity of commitment, success is not far off. Within a few days Mr Binay Rout was counted as one of the most reputed and competent teachers, not only in the school but also in the community of science teachers in the state. He dedicated himself completely for the holistic development of students. He took a lot of care of students, especially students of Class IX and Class

X to prepare them for board examinations. He motivated the students by staying awake with them until late in the night as if students' examinations were really his own examinations. Because of his untiring and sincere efforts, two students from this rural school could figure in the list of top ten in the board examinations in the last two years. When there was so much of pomp and ceremony about the private schools in the state, this unprecedented success of a rural government school was a source of inspiration and encouragement to all. So Binay Sir enjoyed a lot of love and respect among the students and teachers as well. Binay Sir still remembers the lines that Ramakrishna Sir often quotes, "A school does not attain its identity because of the beautiful sky-touching buildings. The competent and resourceful teachers and the successful and high achiever students of a school give it the identity it possesses."

In view of his versatile talent, the teachers of the school had persuaded Binay Sir to apply for the President's Award for Teachers. Binay Sir got the application in time and sent to the Ministry of Human Resource Development, New Delhi with the signature and recommendation of the Headmaster. All teachers had the strong belief that Binay Sir would surely bag the President's Award for Teachers for that year.

On the 10th of August, the Circle Inspector Mr Shyam Sundar rang up Ramakrishna Sir, the Headmaster to inform him that one of his intimate friends working in the Ministry of Human Resource Development, New Delhi had told him about Narenndranath Vidyapeeth in the district of Jagatsinghpur having figured in the list of teachers to be awarded with the President's Award. The names of the teachers would be formally announced two weeks before the Teachers' Day and the successful teachers would be awarded on the Teachers' Day in the Rashtrapati Bhavan (President's Palace). Hearing about this Ramakrishna Sir became restless. Loudly announcing this to all teachers in a loud voice, he moved on towards Binay Sir. At that time Binay Sir was teaching mathematics in Class VII. The Headmaster rushed into the classroom and hugged Binay Sir. "Binay, you have been selected for the President's Award. Be ready to go to Delhi to receive the award." Ramakrishna Sir said all these in one breath. Binay Sir looked at Ramakrisna Sir's face in surprise. Tears rolled down from his eyes. He paid obeisance to Ramakrishna Sir, touched his feet, brought his hands together and put them on his head to seek his blessings. The whole class was spell-bound to witness such an emotionally-charged scene. Blessing him Ramakrishna Sir said, "Okay Binay, please come to the Teachers' Common Room after your class is over. Today the teachers are definitely going to demand a party from me for this wonderful achievement of yours."

There were ripples of happiness all around in the school. Everyone, right from the students to the peons, was overjoyed about this great achievement of Binay Sir. He would have to go to Delhi to receive the award. The President himself would give away the award to him in a splendid ceremony in the Rashtrapati Bhawan on the eve of Teachers' Day. The names of the winners shall be announced in the Television and in the newspapers on the 20th of August. So there was an environment of celebration in the school. Everyone eagerly waited for the news on the television and the newspapers on 20th August when Binay Sir's name would be officially announced as one of the winners.

Twentieth of August was a Saturday. Everyone was waiting for the newspapers to arrive. The newspapers did not reach this rural place early in the morning. It was already 10.30 am when the newspaper reached the school. Teachers were busy in their classes. Only Srihari Sir was inside the Teachers' Common Room. When the peon reached there with the newspaper, Srihari Sir he took the newspaper from him and opened the second page containing the list of teachers from Odisha selected for the President's Award. As he went on reading the names of the schools one after another, he came across the name of Narendranath Vidyapeeth, Punang, Jagatsinghpur. It was such a great news! He could not believe his eyes when he saw the name of the Headmaster Mr Ramakrishna Mishra in place of Mr Binay Rout. Was it a printing mistake? Was the name of the Headmaster printed in place of Mr Binay Rout? He came out on to the verandah with the newspaper. Ramakrishna Sir was teaching in the nearby room. Shrihari Sir rushed to him. Seeing the newspaper in his hands, Ramakrishna Sir also came out of the classroom. Shrihari Sir showed him the newspaper and informed that Binay's name was not there. Within no time, the teachers from all the classrooms came out to see the newspaper. Everyone had the same confusion. Definitely there was some mistake somewhere. The name of the Headmaster of the school had been wrongly printed. Everyone persuaded Ramakrishna Sir to make a call to the Circle Inspector and find out the truth. Just at this time, the telephone in the Teachers' Common Room rang. Everyone along with the Headmaster came rushing to the Teachers' Common Room. The Circle Inspector was on the other side of the phone. He congratulated Ramakrishna Sir and said, "I came to know about it after receiving a fax from Delhi. As a matter of fact, you should have got it much earlier.

You are the pride for this circle as well as this district." On the other end of the phone, Ramakrishna Sir tried to interrupt him and say something but the Circle Inspector went on congratulating him. Finally, the Circle Inspector Shyamsundar Babu put down the phone. Ramakrishna Sir was speechless after hearing this news. He felt himself guilty. Everyone was worried about how such a mistake could occur. He must call either Bhubaneswar or Delhi to confirm the news. He found himself in a dilemmatic situation. What could Binay be thinking right now? He was so hopeful. Having said this, he went on browsing through the pages of the telephone directory.

Just at this time Binay Sir entered the room slowly and silently with his face down. He went straight to the Headmaster, held his legs in tight embrace and wept inconsolably. He said, "Sir, There has not been any mistake anywhere. You yourself have got the award." All the teachers were spellbound and looked at Binay in astonishment. Binay went on speaking, "When the topic of President's Award for Teachers was being discussed, I thought you were the most suitable person. You have not applied for the award till date only because you have never taken it seriously. Hence I had filled in the application for you by mentioning the books written by you, your qualitative publications in the newspapers, the science projects that you have prepared, your innovative style of teaching and your other achievements in teaching and learning that you have at the state level. Moreover, it was necessary for you to sign as the Headmaster of the school. Unknowingly, you too signed in the application form for the award. Sir, it is because of you, your commitment and sacrifice, a poor orphan boy like me has been able to establish himself as a teacher in the society and therefore you deserve it the most. You are the most suitable candidate for this award, not me." Having said this, Binay Sir burst into tears again. By this time, the eyes of Ramakrishna Sir as well as all the teachers present there had started welling up with tears. Ramakrishna Sir lifted Binay up, leaned him against his shoulder, fondly patted on his back and wiped out his tears with the end of his *dhoti* (loin cloth). All other teachers hugged Binay Sir. Ratnakar Sir said, "Really Binay, you are the Ekalavya of our times. Ekalavya only sacrificed his thumb for his teacher to pay the *Guru Dakshina*[3] to his teacher but you have surrendered your heart to your teacher!"

Srihari Sir hugged Ramakrishna Sir and congratulated him. He said, "Sir, whatever Binay says is right. You are not only an expert teacher, a popular writer and an erudite educationist, you are also person who has discovered the erudition, talent and quality in Binay. You have groomed him to reach the place he deserves. We have only helped students in their careers. But you have groomed and reared up a teacher. Hence you are the most suitable person for this award. Binay has a long career ahead. But you are going to retire this year. Hence Binay's efforts are most timely and praiseworthy."

Everyone was delighted to hear what Shrihari Sir said. All were mesmerized by this unique and heart-touching incident. In order to alleviate the seriousness in the environment, Nrusingha Sir said to the Headmaster, "Sir, today a simple tea party won't do. We need a grand celebration. Ramakrishan Sir said, "Absolutely.". When all

---

3 In India it is the tradition in the Gurukuls to repay to one's 'guru' or the 'teacher' after the completion of education for the teachings imparted by them. This is a way of showing respect and gratitude to the teachers or the gurus.

were busy in chit-chatting, Binay Sir was getting ready to go somewhere. Ramakrishna Sir shouted from a distance, "Binay, where are you going in such a hurry?"

Sitting on the bicycle, Binay Sir said, "Sir, I will have to go to Jagatsinghpur Railway Station to reserve a train ticket for your Delhi tour. We may not get a ticket if we are delayed."

Ramakrishan Sir said, "A crazy fellow indeed!"

❑

The Ultimate Decision

The whole school has been active and lively since yesterday. The Headmaster has issued instructions to everybody. The Circle Inspector will visit the school with the competent authorities from Bhubaneswar. Hence the whole campus needs to be cleaned. Children have removed the weeds and unwanted grass to make it clean. However, all these things do not seem to be making any difference to Sudhir. Year before, cleaning the campus was their routine work but after the departure of Arun Sir, all such things had been discontinued and no one seemed to take any interest in these works. Arun Sir used to take so much personal care to clean the campus. He used to remove the grass on his own, watered the pumpkin plants, planted the rows of flower plants near the gate. Watching all these activities today, Sudhir fondly remembers Arun Sir time and again. He turns nostalgic and goes gloomy and disappointed. Two drops of tears cascaded down his cheeks. Leaning against the guava tree planted by Arun Sir, Sudhir got lost in his thoughts. Arun Sir left the school three years ago but has not visited the school since then.

Three years ago Arun Sir joined as an Assistant Teacher in this Primary School in Ichhapur. Having completed his education recently, he had a child-like soft, crystal-clear and innocent mind. But his intelligence, conscience and thoughts were brilliant. Once Sapan, a student of Class V, said in a complaining tone, "Sir, the school of the nearby village has a beautiful building, there are fans in the classrooms and many other facilities but in our school….." .Arun Sir patted Sapan on his back and said, "All these do not matter much. What one needs is strength of mind. With strong will power and strength of mind, teachers and students can realign all odd things in favour of education. Irrespective of the thatched roofed schools, broken furniture or torn and soiled books they use, they can do wonders. All facilities like good buildings, fans, lights, books become worthless and useless, if the students and teachers do not have dedication. The teacher himself is an institution, a school, the books and curriculum, all rolled into one. The solutions to all problems lie inside the teachers as the teacher himself/herself is an institution of learning."

Sudhir heaved a deep sigh. Yes, Sir had said the right thing. It was Arun Sir who solved all the problems in his life.

Sudhir's house was close to the bank of the canal on the other end of the school. His father, a landless farmer, cultivated about one hectare of land on tenant farming. Therefore Sudhir had to help his father in most of the activities related to agricultural farming: planting the seeds, removing the weeds and ploughing the land etc. He used to go to the fields early in the morning with his father. But as soon as the school bell rang at 10 am, he felt restless and could not control himself. He removed the towel tied round his waist and put it over his shoulders. Washing his hands in the muddy water, he ran on the boundaries of the fields and reached the school premises for prayer. Standing at one end of the queue of students, he folded his hands together for prayer just like other students. After the prayer ceremony, students went back to their classes but poor Sudhir returned to his fields with a heavy heart.

Arun Sir observed Sudhir's activities for a few days. He could notice in him an ardent desire for studies. One day, out of curiosity, he asked the Headmaster about Sudhir. The Headmaster said, "Yes, he is a special boy. His name is Sudhir, son of Mr Pahali Nayak, a farmer of this village. Since childhood he has been joining other children for prayer every day. Whenever he gets a chance, he plays with them during recess and reads their books. As soon as he comes across a good sapling, he brings it and plants in the school premises." Arun Sir was spellbound to hear this. He thought that the child must be having some invisible deep attraction for the school. Perhaps the dream of studying in a school made him restless.

One fine morning Arun Sir reached Sudhir's home in the morning. When he talked about Sudhir's interest for school, hisfather said, "Sir, Sudhir has a lot of interest for studies. He procures old books from school children in exchange of mangoes and guavas and reads them at his leisure. I often notice his interest for studies but I am helpless. I cannot do anything for him though I sincerely want. Sir, we are daily wagers. What shall we eat if we don't work for wages? I have taken some land near the school on lease. Sudhir's mother has not been able to work in the fields since she fell ill. Hence Sudhir is my only hope and support whom I can depend upon. So Sir, how can I spare him?"

Arun Sir replied, "Listen Pahali, if Sudhir has so much interest for studies, he can pursue his studies simultaneously while working in the fields. Let him work in the fields for 2-3 hours in the morning and then come to attend classes in the school. After that he can work in the fields again after the recess. I will also teach him in the night for one hour every day. The boy is intelligent. He will do well if he is a given a chance to study." Arun Sir questioningly looked at Sudhir and asked, "Sudhir, can you handle both the responsibilities?" Sudhir was eagerly waiting for an opportunity. Thrilled with excitement, he replied, "Yes Sir, Yes Sir", rushed to Arun Sir and prostrated before him. Noticing this intense interest of Sudhir for studies, Pahali preferred to keep quiet. The next day Sudhir was admitted in Class IV. Arun Sir persuaded many guardians like Pahali to get their wards admitted in the school. He trained children in making small paper pouches out of old books, notebooks and newspapers, carpentry, knitting fishing net etc. . He encouraged the shopkeepers in the village market to use the small and big paper pouches prepared by children instead of the polythene bags to keep the village environment clean.

Arun Sir was a *Karma Yogi*[4] in the true sense of the term. He used to stay in a single roomed thatched house near the school. He too wanted to go for higher studies. He had been dreaming of becoming an OAS (Odisha Administrative Service) Officer some day. But his family

---

4 *As per Lord Krishna's teachings in the Bhagavad Gita, a Karma Yogi is a person who does good to the whole world, loves the whole world and all its beings selflessly. S/He follows the path of righteousness and discharges his duties with utmost sincerity and commitment.*

condition was not supportive enough to prepare for OAS examination. On his shoulders, he had the onus of getting his brothers and sisters educated. So he wanted to become an officer with a higher salary. He read a lot in the dim light until midnight. Soon he cleared the written test for the OAS examinations and was shortlisted for the interview. So he used the day time for school duty and spent sleepless nights for his preparation for the interview. The interview was scheduled after a few days. He also successfully cracked the interview. Afterwards, he was invited to Bhubaneswar for training.

When the news of Arun Sir's selection for OAS spread among all, there was pin drop silence everywhere. All children of the school went silent. Their favourite Arun Sir was going to leave the job in the school to work as an officer in Bhubaneswar. Sudhir gave up eating after hearing this news. Arun Sir was an important page in the book of his life. How could he continue his studies without him? Sudhir was packing the books, clothes and bed roll of Arun Sir. But his face had turned red because of suppressed grief. Arun Sir gave him a fifty rupee note but Sudhir was hesitant. He hugged Arun Sir and wept to his heart's content. There were tears in Arun Sir's eyes as well. Sudhir retained the note when Arun Sir insisted on it. He requested Arun Sir to give his autograph on it. Arun Sir smiled and put a tiny signature on the note. Till date Sudhir has preserved the note with utmost care. In spite of financial hardships, he has never thought of spending and parting with the currency note carrying the imprint of the sweet memories of Arun Sir.

Sudhir was taken aback to hear the horn of a car blowing. Yes, it was a government vehicle which parked near the school gate. The Headmaster Prasanna Sir, the Assistant Teachers Mr Samal, Mr Murmu and others ran towards the gate. Children in the school peeped out of their classroom windows. Sudhir too looked in that direction. He could not believe his eyes. Arun Sir got down from the car. A clerk followed him with the files in his hands. The School Inspector came last in the line. Getting down from the car, Arun Sir first of all saluted Prasanna Sir. Prasanna Sir exclaimed, "Oh, Arun! It's nice to see you here!"

"Yes, Sir. After the probationary training, I have been appointed as the District Project Coordinator of Sarva Shikhya Abhiyan in Bhubaneswar. I was very much interested to visit Ichhapur School since long. So I didn't let this opportunity go out of my hands and came here. The Headmaster said, "You have done the right thing. We and the children miss you a lot."

Arun Sir felt as if had come back to his own home. Pushing everyone aside, he went forward to the classes. Children paid their obeisance to him. This school is a citadel of memory for him. The noise of children, chalk, duster, blackboard- all are familiar to him. Sudhir came running from class Seven. Hugging Arun Sir tightly, he burst into tears.

The official works were completed at around 2 O' clock. Arun Sir and all others had lunch together. Now it was time for his farewell. Sudhir plucked some ripe guavas from the tree, packed them in a carry bag and handed them over to Arun Sir and said, "Sir, the tree that you had planted has started bearing fruits for the first time this year." Arun Sir gave some advice to the crowd of students gathered there. Then he moved towards the gate in the company of teachers. The driver was in a hurry. It would be 5 pm by the time they reached Bhubaneswar. Having reached the gate, Arun Sir threw a last glance at the school premises. He saw the children standing on the veranda, weeping and wiping their tears. Sudhir sat on the Veranda, wept with his head hung between his knees and did not even look up. At this time Arun Sir's eyes caught sight of the marble bust of Gopabandhu near the flag post. While working in the school, he used to clean the bust with a wet cloth every day before prayer. He also engaged students to make an awning of coconut leaves over the bust three to four times in a year. Now the bust looked pale and decayed under the dilapidated awning. It appeared to him as if *Gopabandhu*[5] was saying, "The Hindus are not born for their selfish interests (*nija swartha pain jata nuhen hindu*); Every drop of blood of the Hindus is shed for the welfare of the world (*biswa hite hindu prati rakta bindu*)." Having put his hands inside his packets, he looked downward and stood silently for some time. Looking at the school campus, he asked the peon for a sheet of white paper. Then he put the paper on the bonnet of the car and wrote something on it. Then, handing over the paper to the clerk he said, "Prashant Babu, please take this Letter of Resignation and hand it over to the Education Secretary in the Secretariat. Due to some technical reasons, my resignation from this school has not been accepted yet. I have written in this letter that I will withdraw that Letter of Resignation and will rejoin this school as an Assistant Teacher. Prashant Babu, I cannot live without the school and children."

People present there were dumbfounded. They

---

5 *Gopabandhu Das(1877-1928), popularly known as Utkala-mani Gopabandhu Das, was a social worker, reformer, political activist, journalist, poet and essayist of Odisha, India.*

could not believe what Arun Sir said. Is he really going to abandon such a nice job with such a handsome salary, government quarters, peons, vehicle everything and come back to this school in this rural area? But Arun Sir was a man of exceptional conviction. Intoxicated by his passion and extraordinary commitment for the profession, love and affection for children, Arun Sir did not waver a little in his decision. He remained stable and effulgent like a bright sun and spread a positive vibe in all directions.

Giving out a hearty laugh, Arun Sir proceeded towards the school, as if he was back to his permanent address today. Moving on to the verandah, like a dedicated teacher, he instructed the students, "What are you doing here? Go to your respective classrooms in queue. Ah Sudhir, are you not in a mood to read? Now it is the time for the seventh period. Let's go to the class. Today I will demonstrate a nice experiment from science." Looking up, Sudhir could not believe what he saw with his own eyes. His dear Arun Sir was back to him, standing beside him and asking him to go to the class. With a smile on his lips, he stood up and rushed to his class.

Arun Sir's white government vehicle carried his Letter of Resignation and moved towards Bhubaneswar on the banks of the canal, leaving circles of dust behind.

❑

The Transformative Mentor

It was the month of May 1977. With no pressure of studies or examinations, Abhinab was a free bird. He enjoyed his summer vacation in the company of his wild dreams and his friends, and relatives who visited his village to spend their summer holidays. Starting early in the morning after some snacks, he would move with his friends in and around the village. While inside the village, they would look for guava or custard apple trees to get the ripe fruits, loiter in the mango groves for ripe and raw mangoes, run in the streams flowing by the village, chasing swarms of fish and trying to catch them and trod into the fields with green grams, groundnuts to collect them, boil them and relish eating them with the evening snacks. When there were any guests, Abhinab had a gala time, for two reasons: there was no fear of getting scolded for anything wrong and there were additional delicious items in the menu for lunch and dinner. Immersed in these merry-making and fun-filled activities, he had forgotten all about the scholarship examination that he had appeared a month ago.

On a Saturday morning he was out with his maternal uncle Ramesh to the mango groves to the north of the village. The uncle and nephew duo moved from one tree to another tree, threw stones and sticks at the mangoes to strike down the mangoes from the trees. Ramesh uncle, being city-bred, could not hit the mangoes as skillfully as Abhinab, who was an expert in this. Ramesh uncle succeeded once in ten attempts whereas Abhinab was successful in one out of two attempts. Ramesh uncle patted Abhinab on his back for his expertise in a gesture of appreciation. Abhinab felt happy and elated when Ramesh uncle appreciated him. The Uncle nephew duo could collect 15 mangoes as a result of 2 hours of hard work. As they did not have a bag to carry the mangoes, they carried the mangoes with the long stalks in their hands. Abhinab took out his shirt and tied it round his waist. Then he put the rest of the mangoes in the part of the shirt dangling from his waist and tied it. In this avatar, he looked like the son of a watchman of a mango grove.

Just when both of them reached Abhinab's home, Abhinab's father had come back from school and was parking his bicycle in the cycle stand. As he had come in the scorching heat of summer, his face had turned red and he was sweating profusely. When he saw Abhinab in his rustic avatar, he was furious. Abhinab had thought that he would be spared as he was accompanied by Ramesh uncle. But he was not that lucky. Ramesh uncle was not on the scene as he had been to Abhinab's uncle's house and poor Abhinab had to bear the brunt of his father's anger alone. Without saying anything, his father pulled out a bamboo stick from the thatched cowshed in front of their home and started thrashingAbhinab black and blue. Abhinab could not make head and tail of this merciless act of his father. He started howling in pain and ran towards his mother. His mother tried her best to save him from his father but she could not. Rather she got beaten a couple of times. However, with consistent efforts, she was able to stop him from his aggressive attack on Abhinab. When she tried to know the reason, he started explaining, "This fellow has spoiled my name and fame. He got scholarship in Class III and Class V. I was sure that he would also get scholarship in class VII. But he has not qualified for the scholarship. How can we expect him to get a scholarship when he indulges in such idiotic habits? Look at his face. Looks like an illiterate boy from the slums. Look at what he has done to his shirt! He has converted the shirt into a bag to carry the mangoes. I changed his school last year with the hope that he would read well and qualify in the scholarship. But I was a fool to think like that. This fellow is good for nothing. I am going to take out his Transfer Certificate from the school and engage him in the fields." He said all these in one breath and sat down out of frustration.

Abhinab's mother took him to the other room, out of his father's sight. The purple impressions of the bamboo stick were clearly visible on his hands, back, buttocks and thighs. There were bruises in a couple of places as well. He was writhing in pain, agony and frustration. His mother caressed the wounds with her affectionate hands and applied balm on those places. She also served him food in his room though usually they all had lunch together. He could not understand why he did not qualify in the examination. To the best of his knowledge, he had fared well in the examination but the results were surprising and disappointing. The whole world seemed to be full of darkness for him. He was sad not because he had not qualified in the scholarship examination but because he was not even given a chance to explain his position.

In the afternoon Abhinab did not go out. He lay in one corner of his study room and did not talk with anyone in the family. His sisters came close to him, touched his wounds, empathized with him and sat beside him. They tried to comfort him and assuage his grief. That day he had his dinner early before everybody and went to sleep. Though he tried to sleep, he could not. The pain in different parts of his body did not let him sleep properly. Moreover, thoughts about his future kept haunting him. He visualized himself working in the fields with the farmers or mending the cattle with the cowboys like the other boys of his age from the village. He was frightened by these disturbing thoughts. However, after midnight, the balm that his mother had applied on the bruises gave him some relief from the pain and he could sleep for some time.

The next day was a Sunday. He decided not to go before anybody. He was afraid that everyone would talk about the results of the scholarship examination, which would add salt to his injuries. He did not go before his father as he was scared of being reminded of his failure and abused again. He did not go out for the fear of being ridiculed by his friends who had discouraged him from fillingin the application for scholarship. His close friends came right at 9 am to call him for the holiday errands that they used to engage in but his mother told them that he was not keeping well and did not allow them to meet him. She did not want them to know that he had been thrashed black and blue by his father for not qualifying in the scholarship examination. Sitting alone in his room Abhinab looked at the books of Class VII lying on his table, gathering dust since the examinations were over. He dusted off the books carefully with a piece of cloth and put them back on the table. Had he given a little more attention to his books instead of merry-making, he would not have faced this day today. But now all the roads were closed for him. He could not undo the damages that he had already caused. When he was engrossed in all these thoughts, his mother called him for lunch.

Abhinab kept himself away from others for a couple of days, until his father called him one day and sharedthe plan that he had designed for him. He informed Abhinab that he should apply for the National Rural Talent Search Examination and prepare under the mentorship of Shri Bir Kishore Das, Headmaster of the PSME School from which he had completed class VII. At first he could not understand his plan as the school was one and half kilometers away from his village. While studying in that school he used to walk to the school every day in the morning and come back in the evening. Moreover, there was no hostel in the school. But his father made everything clear for him. He said that the next day he would personally take him to the school and make arrangements for his stay in the school premises from that day onward. Every day, he would have to pack his bag immediately after coming from school and go to Dash Sir, stay there in the school in the night under his care and supervision and return early in the morning the next day. His mother tried to interrupt and advocate for Abhinab. She said that for a boy of his age it would be a challenge and might often invite trouble for the family but his father was adamant. He said that he had already discussed the matter with Dash Sir and he had kindly agreed to mentor him for the National Rural Talent Search Examination to be held in the month of August. Abhinab had no scope to raise any protest. Moreover, he had lost the moral right to raise any objection to any decision. On second thought, he thought that it might be God's plan to test his talent and perseverance. Perhaps God wanted to give him an opportunity to prove his talent.

The next day his father took Abhinab to the school on his bicycle. He carried a small bed roll and a few items that he would require during his stay in the school. Mother also gave Abhinab his dinner packed in a Tiffin carrier. Abhinab was excited for the new but challenging experience. They reached the school at around six pm. When they reached the school, Dash Sir was waiting for them in his room. He showed them a small room with a bed where Abhinab had to stay. From the conversation between his father and Dash Sir, Abhinab could gather that Dash Sir was equally disappointed over his failure and considered it to be his personal failure. Hence he had agreed to put in all sincere efforts to guide Abhinab for the NRTS examination. After a few minutes' discussion, Abhinab's father left him in the school and went away. Abhinab promised to himself that he would put his heart and soul together to deliver his best in the examination. He could see a great difference between his father and Dash Sir. One was angry, emotional, impatient, reactive, talkative and the other was cool, rational, patient, understanding and a man of few words. Abhinab considered himself lucky to have got the mentorship of Dash Sir.

Right from day one, Dash Sir shared his plan of completing the syllabus within a short period of time with Abhinab. He told him clearly that they had only two months at their disposal and they had to achieve the goal by all means. He further cautioned him that he might be required to burn the midnight oil on many nights. Then Dash Sir handed over the daily schedule of study that he had so meticulously prepared. He also apprised him of the mode of study that he would be following. Abhinab would go through the lessons prescribed for the day in the first two hours and he would give him the tasks on the lessons before dinner. He would complete the tasks after dinner,before going to bed. Early morning would be devoted to working on the sums from mathematics. This routine planned by Dash Sir suited Abhinab as he too usually did the same before the examinations. In course of time the relationship between Abhinab and Dash Sir grew intense. Dash Sir enjoyed teaching Abhinab and Abhinab enjoyed being groomed and mentored by Dash Sir.

Dash Sir monitored Abhinav's progress on a day-to-day basis and cautioned him when he noticed any erratic behavior or decreasing performance on the part of Abhinab. He visited Abhinab's room at regular intervals to ensure that he did not engage in any distracting activities or he did not fall asleep before time. Dash Sir also knew that for a young boy of 12, coming to him every day in the evening, going back in the morning next day and then again getting ready for school was a great challenge but he did not want to let the opportunity go out of his hand. Moreover, he had strong confidence in the intelligence and ability of Abhinab.

Abhinab was deeply influenced by the life style and commitment of Dash Sir. Dash Sir got up early in the morning. After finishing his daily chores, he would come to his room at 5 am and help him work out the sums from the books. He never explained anything to him directly. He helped Abhinab do them on his own. He just provided the tips. He prepared his own food before the school started. He did not let the school peon do any of the household works for him. In spite of all these commitments, he was always the first employee of the school to attend office. All through the day he did not have a single minute's rest, except for the time for lunch break that he used to take his lunch. He would go to the classes, observe the teachers taking the classes and was always ready to take the classes wherever there were no teachers or teachers were on leave. The teachers were amazed to see his level of agility and depth of knowledge. There was no subject which he could not teach. Being soft-spoken and knowledgeable, he was everyone's favourite. In the afternoon, after the school was over, he would lie down on his bed for half an hour and then go out for evening walk for half an hour. Then he was again back to his busy personal life. During this period, he had now accommodated Abhinab's schedule. Abhinab could not help admiring such a great personality who had taken responsibility for a student like him.

The same was the case with Abhinab. He tried to deliver his best to match the hard work put in by his beloved mentor Dash Sir. He could not remember the day when he had a full sound sleep of 6 hours or more. He could not remember when he had taken a hot delicious meal last time. His mother was very much worried for him. She could not serve him hot lunch or dinner, not even on Sundays but she was happy that Abhinab was finally on the right track. She prayed Lord Jagannath that her son should come out successful in the examination. Abhinab made most of his waking hours and dedicated them to his studies so that he did not have to repent again. He was hopeful that he would be able to live up to the expectations of his father and Dash Sir.

Under the guidance and mentorship of Dash Sir, Abhinab went on improving in his behavior and performance by leaps and bounds. He had learnt two big lessons in life: small mistakes often lead to big disasters and one's immediate environment decides what one can do. Dash Sir was also very much satisfied with his progress and was very hopeful that Abhinab would come out with flying colours in the NRTS examination. He told Abhinab's father that Abhinab was doing well and he was optimistic about his success.

Two months elapsed in this manner. Neither Dash Sir nor Abhinab could keep track of the rapid passage of time. Finally, the much-awaited day arrived. Abhinab had to go to the nearest cityto appear the NRTS examination. He was accompanied by Shri Dinamani Mishra, one of the senior teachers of the school. Mishra Sir took every care of Abhinab and ensured that he did not have any trouble either before or during the examinations.

In the Examination Hall, Abhinab was scared to see so many competitors and became a little nervous. Just at this moment he recollected the words that his father had used on the day of declaration of the results of the scholarship examination. He visualized himself planting the seedlings in the fields, minding the cattle in the forests, so on and so forth. Then he remembered his own sacrifice as well as the sacrifice for the goal that he and Dash Sir had set together. He focused his attention on the examination and started attempting the questions one after another. He was unaware when the examination was over. When the last bell rang, he was answering the last question. He requested the teacher to allow him half a minute and finished the answer. When he came out, Dinamani Sir was eagerly waiting for him to know about his performance in the examination. The reputation of his school depended upon his performance. He was very happy when he came to know about Abhinab's good performance.

Reaching home, Abhinab told his parents about his good performance in the examination. His father was happy that his decision to send him to Bir Kishore Dash Sir was a right decision. His mother was happy that Abhinab would not have to spend nights outside and take so much pain. But Abhinab was back to his natural self. He was again a free bird, back in the company of his friends doing the same old things that they did together before his special coaching period for the NRTS examination. His father allowed him this liberty as he felt that Abhinab should be given some freedom after all hard work that he had put in during the last two months.

On another Saturday in September, Abhinab was learning riding bicycle with his friends on the state highway. He had forgotten all about the entrance examination for the NRTS scholarship that he had appeared a month ago. Just at this time, one of his teachers from the nearby village Shri Badri Narayan Rath was going to his village from the school through the same route. When he saw Abhinab, he got down from his bicycle and congratulated him. Abhinab could not make any head or tail of it. When he asked the reason for this, Ratha Sir handed over a small chit of paper. The paper read, "Abhinab Mishra First Kamanaguda Block." Abhinab touched the feet of his teacher in obeisance and then ran towards home. His father's joy knew no bounds when he came to know about this. He announced it before everyone in the village.

Next Monday Abhinab's father went straight to the PSME School, hugged Dash Sir and profusely thanked him for his selfless sacrifice and transformative mentorship during the entire period. He announced before all the staff that he would throw a party for all on the next Wednesday for this achievement of his son. Abhinab touched the feet of all his teachers and sought their blessings for success in life. Dash Sir tightly hugged Abhinab and patted him on his back. It was a historic day for him as this was for the first time that a student of his school had bagged the first prize in the NRTS Examination. For Dash Sir it was a personal achievement as he had never ever dedicated so much of his time and energy for a single student in his entire teaching career. Thus started a life-long relationship between the Dash Sir and Abhinab, the Guru and Shishya of modern times.

❑

Exotic Bonding

After completing B.Ed, I started my teaching career as a teacher in a Government Girls' High School in Phulbani District of Odisha. I was in a dilemma whether I should join the job or not as it was far away from Bhubaneswar. However, after consulting my friends and seniors, I decided to join there. It was a very old school with a student strength of nearly 800. The student population included children of the local tribal people, some government employees and some local businessmen. Within no time I got familiar with the school. Located at the feet of a mountain and surrounded by teak and other flowering trees, the school looked cool and serene in the hide and seek of sunlight and shade. Moreover, as the school was located in a rural and remote area, the students of this school were very soft, honest and innocent. I was also lucky to get accommodation inside the school premises. This way I started my career as a teacher with a lot of thrill and excitement. The thrill or excitement of a new job is something unique, rare and different. I had the pluck to beat a million odds to hit at the target.

Students of this school were very lovely and sensitive. With their young minds filled with adolescent agility, creativity and innovativeness, they got involved with their heart and soul together when they were motivated to do something. As I was a new teacher, I had been given the responsibility of taking care of many other co-curricular assignments, in addition to teaching. Therefore I had formed a special group of young girls, including Ishani and Neelima, two students from Class VIII, to assist me in these works. They had keen interest and commitment in everything: right from studies to organizing, participating in and managing various activities. Ishani was fair and slim with bright dazzling eyes. She was very rational and systematic in everything she did. Neelima was slightly dark in complexion and was well known for her long thick braids. She was very creative and imaginative. Ishani's father, originally from Baripada, was an officer in the Union Bank of India. But Nilima's father was a permanent resident of Phulbani, running a furniture business. Ishani and Neelima were very intimate and perfectly complemented each other in everything. They were my only close companions in my solitary life. Very often they used to come to my residence. I spent my time comfortably and constructively in teaching them, training them in song and dance and preparing the teaching materials with their support. During the Ganesh Puja, Saraswati Puja and Annual Functions, my house became the workshop for children.

I was enraptured by the intimacy between Ishani and Neelima. Once I asked them, "How did you become so intimate?" Ishani replied, "Madam, our relationship is very deep. We have been like this since the day we met each other three years ago. Our friends and teachers know us as 'The Perfect Pair' and cite our example when they discuss friendship. We cannot spend a single day without each other. We were connected to each other even before we met each other. Look, her name in Odia starts with the letter that my name ends with."

"Oh! That sounds interesting," I said.

Neelima cut in and said, "Madam, I would like to say something provided that you don't get angry." Encouraging her, I assured, "Please go ahead."

"Madam, your name starts with the letter that my name ends with and Ishani's name starts there where your name ends."

I said with a smile, "Oh really! You have done so much of research meanwhile to explore such formulations.

The simple equation involving our names excited me much that day. I could not help appreciate the creativity and smartness of both the girls. Back home, I thought of the deep bond of friendship between them. My relationship with them grew stronger with the passage of time. In course of time, I discovered that the duo spent most of the time in the school in the company of each other and did everything together. They even prepared for the inter-class competitions and examinations together. Both of them were very good at studies but were never jealous of each other. They had the mission of boosting and grooming each other and growing together. As their teacher and mentor, I too wanted them to shine in everything and become role models for their juniors. I closely monitored their scholastic and co-scholastic activities and ensured their progress in the right direction.

My first year of stay got completed successfully. Now both Nilima and Ishani were in Class IX and showed great interest in their studies. They were also very punctual in their attendance in the school. After some days I noticed that Ishani was not regular in the school as before. I did not have the contact number of Ishani's parents. Out of anxiety, one day I asked Neelima outside the class, "Neelima, What's the matter with Ishani? I don't see her in the school nowadays."

-Madam, don't you know that she has not been keeping well for a long time? She is seriously ill; I don't know what to do. I miss her everywhere in the school. In the prayer class, in the classroom, during recess, at the lunch table, in the playground… .everywhere…always …

-Neelima dear, I can very much understand your feelings. You both are so much attached to each other. I too miss her a lot. I can't throw a glance at you in the class because I don't see her beside you. Whenever I look at you, she comes to my mind. Nowadays I also notice that you are not able to focus on your studies as before.

-Madam, how can I study when my partner is not with me? We are just two bodies but one soul. Her absence tears my soul apart and I cannot focus on anything, let alone studies. Sometimes I feel that I will go mad if she continues remaining absent from the school.

- By the way, did you ever find any scope to ask her parents about her disease?

-No, Madam. I haven't dared to ask that. I can't. Her parents are so disheartened and upset about her illness. They may not be willing to tell me something unpleasant and dishearten me.

-Dear, it has been more than a month that she has not come to the school. Let's visit her house someday and find out her whereabouts.

-Madam, that will be the right thing.

-Yes dear, we'll visit her house at this weekend.

-Thank you, Madam.

On Sunday I carried some fruits and biscuits and went to Ishani's house in the company of Neelima. We were shocked to see Ishani. She looked very weak and pale, beyond recognition. Neelima went close to her, caressed her head and hugged her tightly. She told Ishani that she missed her very much. Ishani said, "I too miss you dear. I wish I got well soon." Having said this, she looked blankly at Neelima but did not say anything. Her bright eyes had turned lusterless and were full of tears. When Ishani's father greeted us, I asked him, "Good morning, Sir, is Ishani alright? She has not been coming to school for a long period. We miss her a lot in the school."

Her father replied, "No Madam, she has been suffering from intermittent fever for the last one month."

"Have you been able to diagnose her disease?" I asked.

"No madam, not yet. We have tried all kinds of clinical tests but the cause of her fever has not been identified yet. We are planning to take her to Cuttack tomorrow," her father replied.

In a tone of assurance I said, "Yes, Sir. That will be the best choice. SCB Medical College in Cuttack has all modern facilities for test and treatment. Please let me know if I can be of any help during your stay in Cuttack."

Before leaving her, I comforted Ishani and her father. It was also a tough task for me to convince Neelima. She kept herself cool and controlled in front of Ishani to give her strength and courage to bear with tough times but immediately after coming out, she hugged me and broke down. While comforting her, I said, "Look Neelima, you don't have to worry at all. There are expert doctors in SCB Medical College, Cuttack. They can diagnose her disease easily by conducting various tests and start immediate treatment. Just see, she will be alright in a week's time and will be back to school. Nearly a month elapsed but Ishani was not to be seen in the school. Both me and Neelima were restless. Neelima requested me time and again to contact Ishani's father and tell her Ishani's condition. I could guess that Ishani was suffering from some serious disease which required regular treatment but I could not guess what it could be.

One day I went to the Union Bank of India and got the mobile number of Ishani's father. I called him with a lot of excitement but what I heard from him made a shiver run down my whole body. Ishani had been diagnosed with cancer. She was being treated in the Tata Memorial Hospital in Mumbai and had been given chemotherapy for treatment. He could not even say how long they would be required to stay in Mumbai. This news of Ishani shattered my peace of mind so much that I could not sleep all night. Ishani's beautiful smiling face danced before my mind's eyes when I thought of her. I could not find any rhyme and reason why an innocent young girl like her should go through this painful experience. I wondered how I would be able to face Neelima the next day when she would ask me about her health. The next day I remained disturbed in the school and could not concentrate on anything properly. My colleagues were surprised to see my awkward behavior. When I saw Neelima at a distance in the corridor, I hurriedly entered the Staff Common Room to avoid direct encounter with her. I didn't have the courage to face her initially. Neelima would be devastated when she would come to know about this. Her studies would also be seriously affected. But gradually I reconciled to the situation and told myself that I should be strong enough to face the truth and remain calm and stable at that critical hour. I decided to keep this information a secret and not to share this news with anyone, not even with Neelima. It was very painful for me but I had to go through it as there was no other way out. At night, before going to bed, I prayed Almighty Lord Jagannath with folded hands to bless Ishani with a long life and help her get well soon.

Exactly after two months one day Ishani's father called me to inform that doctors had advised to take Ishani home as she was getting somewhat better. As her disease had been diagnosed at the right time and treatment started at an early stage, all were optimistic about her quick recovery. She was back to Phulbani and would go to school from the next day. My joy knew no bounds when I came to know that Ishani was recovering from the disease. Out of happiness and excitement I said, "That's a wonderful news for all of us. Let her come back to school. Engrossed in her studies and being in the company of her friends, she would surely become normal in a few days." I assured her father that I would take her personal care and responsibility in the school.

The next day as usual Ishani came to school with Neelima. Ishani had changed beyond recognition. She had turned into just a skeleton. Her eyes had gone deep into the cavities and looked black. Losing all her hair, she had become bald. I knew that chemotherapy brings about all these changes in one's body but I had never thought that she would be going through such a drastic change within a couple of months. I shivered at her sight but I could not say anything to her. Trying to divert her attention, I said, "Ishani, Welcome back to school. You don't have to worry about your studies at all. I will teach you all the topics that you have missed so far. You can also refer to Neelima's notebooks if you need. Please tell me if you feel weak and uncomfortable. You may go to my residence to take rest if you want any rest."

Ishani's friends surrounded her and volleyed her with many questions. Which disease is she suffering from? Why did she go to Mumbai? Why has she lost all her hair? She was disturbed with all these questions. Neelima felt that all these questions were irrelevant. Annoyed with all these students, she yelled at them and even tried to drag Ishani out of the crowd of students. She was so much disturbed inside by the deteriorating health of her friend that she could not tolerate anyone causing her any pain. I noticed all these things from a distance. I advised the girls, "Look girls, now Ishani is very weak. She needs sufficient rest. The doctor has advised her to speak less. So don't talk much with her." I advised the girls to avoid talking with Ishani but I myself wanted her to be with me under my care and responsibility because besides being a student, she is also one my close companions in my private life. I requested Neelima to take care of Ishani and facilitate her safe return from the school every day.

The next day the Headmistress assigned me with a special responsibility. I had to scrutinize the applications of the SC/ST girls for scholarship and submit them in the Block Office. As the work required focused attention and utmost care, I had to work in isolation in a separate room until the work was completed and then rushed to the Block Office to submit the applications before the office closed. Having been exhausted all day, I went home straightaway from the Block Office and could not meet Ishani or Neelima the whole day. Back in my residence I refreshed myself, changed clothes, prepared a cup of tea and came to the drawing room. When I was about to sit down on the sofa, I could see Ishani and Neelima coming towards my residence from a distance. It was already dusk. I wondered why these girls had not gone home until that time. They had schoolbags on their backs. Hand in hand, they both came towards my house with their faces down. Ishani looked very pale and weak today. Neelima too had put on a scarf over her head. I wondered, "Does she too have some illness? What's the disease she is suffering from? Has she got cold or fever?" With all these thoughts in mind, I opened the front door. They came and stood in the drawing room, leaning against the wall with their heads down.

Asking them to take their seats on the sofa I said, "Instead of going to your homes, what are you doing here at this hour?" Your parents will be worried." Both of them did not say anything in reply and stood quiet for some time. But one could clearly see the dazzle of the tear drops coming down their cheeks. Perplexed I asked, "Is there anything serious? Why are you silent?"

Then Ishani forcefully removed the scarf from Neelima's head and said, "Ma'am, just see what Neelima has done for me." I was taken aback to see Neelima's bald head. "What's the problem? Why have you shaved your head bald like this? You looked so graceful with your beautiful long braids. Who has shaved you bald like this?" I shouted at her. Neelima burst into tears and said, "Madam, I myself got my head shaved to become bald to look like Ishani. Yesterday everyone was calling her 'baldie' and made fun of her, laughed at her and ridiculed her. I could see her agony-stricken face when others behaved with her in this inhuman manner. I could not tolerate all that Madam. I wanted to yell at everybody and slap them for treating Ishani in this manner but I could not. Therefore I decided to become bald so that Ishani gets the moral support from me and doesn't feel embarrassed to be bald. Ma'am, she has already gone through a lot of pain. I don't want her to undergo any pain and become unhappy anymore. I have taken this bold decision because I want to share the suffering, ridicule and humiliation with Ishani and want her to feel that she is not alone in her agony or embarrassment."

I could not believe my eyes and ears. I sat down on the sofa and pulled both of them close to me. I have often seen Neelima showcasing her long cascading tresses on the days of festivals and girls envying her. She was so proud of them but now she has parted with them completely. The girl has such high and mature thoughts at this young age! In our times, when everyone is dying for their selfish interests, this girl has set an example of an exemplary friendship. What a great sacrifice! At this age of adolescence girls take so much care of their hair and bodies to look beautiful but this girl has decided to go bald and look ugly just for the sake of her friend! I have seen many ideals of friendship but this one is one of the rarest. Heart-touching emotions. I asked her, "Neelima, do your parents know about it?" Neelima kept quiet. Ishani said, "No Madam, she hasn't told anyone about this at home. Today she came half an hour before time from home for the school and got her head shaved in the 'New Fashion' Beauty Parlour. Initially, the hairstylist in the saloon could not understand what she instructed. He thought that she wanted to style her hair to get a modern look but he was dumbfounded when she informed him that she wanted a complete head shave. He tried to dissuade her but Neelima insisted on getting her head shaved. The man hesitated at first to cut and shave the thick tresses which he used to style in different ways. But she convinced him with the argument that she had a lot of lice in her head and her mother had asked her to shave her head so that the hair would grow newly. Now she is scared of going home as she might be scolded for this."

I wiped Neelima's tears, hugged her and kissed on her bald head. I said with pride, "Neelima, you have set an example for girls of your age. You have shown to the world that physical beauty hardly matters when the beauty of the soul takes over. This sacrifice of yours will inspire the young generation to fight for better causes. We are proud of you, dear."

Neelima said, "Madam, when my tresses cascaded down and hit the floor of the parlour with the first stroke of the razor, my heart shattered into a million pieces as they were my dearest but when I visualized Ishani's bald head and her agony-stricken face while being humiliated and called 'baldie', I gained strength and restrained myself from any emotional outburst."

"Bravo! Wonderful!" I said to her with a note of encouragement and appreciation. "Madam, I am grateful to God for having blessed me with a friend like Ishani who can read my mind and respond to the palpitations of my soul."

When we were engrossed in our conversation, Ishani's father and Neelima's father together reached my residence, looking for them. They heard everything from me. I was afraid that Neelima's father would be annoyed with her but

I couldn't help appreciate the empathetic approach that he had towards the issue just like his daughter. Hugging his daughter tightly he said, "My darling, Girls like you who can empathize with others in their grief and suffering are very rare. You have made me proud. I am extremely happy. To hell with this hair! This hair hardly matters. No matter whether you have your braids or not. Even without your braids, you are beautiful. You are a queen of sacrifice. Let's go home. You don't have to be scared of your mother. I will convince her."

I was amazed to see the quality of conscience that prevailed in the mind of a semi-literate businessman. I tied the scarf over Neelima's head again. I pulled out a scarf from the box inside my house and tied it over Ishani's head as well. Now they both looked alike. The two friends hugged each other. My eyes welled up with tears of happiness. The farewell scene of the two girls holding their father's hands made me speechless and enthralled. The experience left a deep indelible impression on the canvas of my mind.

❏

Life Beyond Books

Every year students of Regional Institute of Education, Bhubaneswar (RIE), our teacher training institute go for practice teaching for two months to different schools in Bhubaneswar. This helps them gain experience of teaching in the real classroom situations. The members of faculty visit the respective schools to evaluate the teaching of the teacher trainees assigned to them. As usual, a team of our trainees had gone to Capital High School for this training. I had been entrusted with the responsibility of evaluating their teaching.

I engaged Prabhu, my favourite auto-rickshaw driver as usual to take me to the school and bring me back every day. When I go to schools to supervise the trainees, Prabhu becomes happy and says, "Now Madam will go to school every day like children, with a school bag and water bottle." He also enjoys visiting the schools with me one by one. Visit to the schools once in a year also makes me happy. Among the young girls clad in sky-blue uniforms, I try to discover the girl in me forty years ago.

I observe that Prabhu gets more excited when I visit Capital High School. Instead of dropping me at the school gate, he goes inside the premises and parks the auto under a tree. Even after I get down, he keeps sitting in the auto for some time, looks both ways and then leaves the place.

As per schedule, our trainees were to teach in Capital High School from 2.30 pm. I had to sit inside the classroom and evaluate their teaching competence. After Prabhu dropped me there, I moved towards the school in a hurry. Prabhu called me from behind in a soft voice. I looked back. Prabhu came to me and said, "Madam, I have a request." Encouraging him I said, "Please tell me." Prabhu said, "Please do me a favour in exchange of today's fare." I could not understand what he was trying to say. Why won't he take the fare? What could be the request? Pabhu said, "Madam, I was a student of this school. I dropped out from the school, from studies when I was in Class IX. I earnestly want to go round the school and have a close look at it. Whenever I bring you to this school, I fondly remember those old school days. Could you please take me inside the school? Now I am an auto driver. Will these people allow me to go round the premises of the school and see it to my heart's content? If only I could enter the campus with you, I could see the classrooms I had abandoned long ago."

I felt pity for him. How much fascination he has for the school! He has dropped out of the school but has not been able to give up his love for the school. I felt very compassionate for him. I said, "Now you may go. I will talk with the Headmistress and get her permission to take you round the school. I will have taken the permission by the time you come back to pick me up after the school is closed."

I evaluated the teaching of two of the teacher trainees. Then I went to meet the Headmistress. Coincidentally Mrs Sanghamitra Dash, Headmistress was an alumnus of RIE.

She had a lot of respect for our teachers. She stood up in deference to me as soon as she saw me. I said, "You don't have to stand up. Please get seated and continue your work. I am going to make an unusual request, an emotional appeal. Please permit if it is possible." Sanghamitra was worried. "Madam, please tell me. I will surely try." Then I told her about Prabhu's eagerness and interest for seeing the school. Sanghamitra said, "Madam, I have absolutely no problem in this matter. The class scheduled for the last period has been cancelled. There is a meeting of teachers for the half-yearly examinations. Hence there would be no one in the classrooms after the classes are over. Your auto driver can leisurely see the classrooms on the ground floor as well as upper floors."

I said, "Good. I can also accompany him and have a close look at the school. This is a very old and famous school."

Prabhu reached the school at the right time to pick me up. I went to him and brought him along with me. His eyes were gleaming in happiness. At first, he visited the classrooms of the elementary section on the ground floor. Then he took me to the library at the end of the verandah. I too did not know earlier that the school had such a rich and beautiful library. There were so many old books in the library. But half of the space had been occupied with the books received from the government, to be distributed among the students free of cost. Resultantly many good collections of old books lay neglected and scattered here and there. Prabhu recollected his school days when each one of them was allowed to borrow one story book to read during the library period. When I asked him to recall and tell me the name of a book he had borrowed, he quickly remembered borrowing the book *Uncle Tom's Cabin* from the library and reading it. I was delighted to know that Prabhu had not forgotten the name and contents of the book. Then we went upstairs where he showed me each of the rooms, to the left of the staircase. Then he said, "Now the floor is tiled. In our time the floor was cemented. Then he went to the second class room on the right and stopped there for some time. "This Netaji Room was Class IX. This is the classroom from which I had dropped out of the school." Entering the classroom, he touched the blackboard, all benches and desks and walls of the classroom gently. Sitting on a bench near the window side he said, "Madam, this was my seat. I used to sit here all through the year." Pointing to the ground outside the window he said, "Madam, please have a look at the playground. What a huge playground! No school in Bhubaneswar has a playground as large as this! I used to play football well. It is in this playground that I played in state level tournaments. When I remember those days, I am equally happy and repentant. The happiness I derive in remembering those days is in no way less than the repentance I experience."

Out of curiosity, I asked, "Why did you leave school in Class IX? You were a good student, doing well in studies. Heaving a deep sigh he said, "Would you like to listen to my story, Madam? The story of my agony?" Having said this, he dragged the teacher's chair and asked me to sit on it. Then sitting on the narrow bench of students, he went on narrating his bygone days with tearful eyes. I too continued sitting there with interest, attention and patience to listen to the story of struggle of a remorseful student.

Prabhu started, "Madam, we lived in the slums along the railway lines in Bomikhal area. My father used to pull a Trolley and mother worked on wages. As my sister was older than me, she was married by that time and I was the only child at home. I was very obedient and disciplined and did well in my studies since my childhood days. My father wanted me to be a matriculate by all means. As there was no one at home, I often helped my mother in household chores. Sometimes my parents went out to work early in the morning. Hence I had to cook, serve my own meals, eat the food, clean the utensils and then go to school. Though I didn't stand first or second in the class, I used to figure in the list of top ten students in both the sections. Everything was going on smoothly. One day, returning from school I saw that the Municipal officials had pulled down the houses in our slum with a bulldozer and JCB. We often received notices for the demolition of the houses but such notices were mostly not carried out later. But this time they had demolished our houses without any prior notice. Mother had gone out to work and father had been suffering from malaria for the previous four days. By the time mother came rushing after hearing the news of demolition of our slum, our house had already been pulled down. Our articles of daily use, my books and clothes etc. were lying scattered on the road and were being trampled down by the passersby. I was in Class IX at that time. I cried aloud at the sight of all these things. It was the month of August and it was raining cats and dogs. Drenched in rain, father, mother and me together gathered our utensils, boxes, clothes and put them under a large polythene sheet pulled over the damaged plot of land. The earthen oven was full of water. We felt as if the heavens were falling upon us. We didn't know where to stay and what to eat. After getting drenched in rain, father got high fever. In the evening we lit a lantern and all sat together under the polythene sheet. Our world had crumbled down before us. Pondering over where to go and what to eat, parents got restless. No one had eaten anything all day. As father was suffering from fever, he had not eaten properly for the last four days. I asked mother, "What shall we eat? The earthen oven is filled with water. The bundle of wood that we had is floating in water." We had a kerosene stove at home. As it was in a higher place, it had not been damaged. Mother said, "Give me the Kerosene tin. Let me borrow some kerosene from Shankar's house. We shall cook rice on the stove." Father was sitting quiet with his head hung between his knees. Mother went out to borrow kerosene. After half an hour, she came back and sat down hopelessly as Shankar's mother had declined having kerosene. We thought, "When all the people of the slum are in distress, who would help others?" I asked my mother to sit beside father and take his care. Then I dusted off and stood up to do something about it. I felt that something had to be done for all of us: my sick and hungry father who had not eaten properly for the last four days, my tired and hungry mother who had been working restlessly all day and me, the hungry school- returned boy who had only some rice meal in the morning before leaving for school. I had to satiate the hunger of three people by all means. I took the lantern from mother and looked at the thatched roof on the other side. I had brought a terracotta oven from the exhibition ground last year. Luckily it was in a working condition and was usable as it had not been broken. I put it under the tin roof hanging from the damaged wall. I took the umbrella, got a pot full of water from the tube well and put it on the oven. But what could I use as the fuel? I threw my glance in all directions. My eyes caught sight of the old books, note books, prize books of Class VII and VIII. I put rice and potato in the vessel. I got the packet of Class

VII, started tearing off the pages one after another and put them to fire. That could help me boil only the water. Then I burnt the old books, note books, prize books of Class VIII. That could help me only half boil the rice and potato. I was dying out of anger and hunger. I lost my sense of reasoning. I rushed and brought the school bag containing the new books of Class IX and burnt all of them to make the fire burn brighter. The rice and potato got soft and edible only after I had burnt all the books. I held the school bag close to my bosom and broke down out of grief and helplessness. Studies, books and future dreams -all seemed worthless in the teeth of hungry stomachs and agony of hunger.

I served hot rice and potato chutney to my parents. I had a deep sense of gratification when I saw them eating food with contentment. But madam, I could not eat that food as I had prepared that by burning my adorable text books. I drank a small pot of water from the tube well and went to sleep.

The next day I put all the broken furniture, clothes, utensils, on the trolley that father used to pull every day. As father had become very weak, I asked him sit on the trolley. Mother pushed it from the back. I rolled down the trolley and brought it to another slum in Salia street where my uncle lived. I started working in the garage of an acquaintance of my uncle. Afterwards parents became so weak and ill that they could not work. So I had the responsibility of running the family on my shoulders. After learning how to drive an auto and obtaining a license, I am now driving an auto of my owner. I have never had another opportunity to think of studies anymore. But when I look at the school my mind starts revolting. I cry in despair and futility."

When his story was about to end, the school peon

reached there and said, "Madam, Hope you have seen all the rooms. Shall I lock the classrooms now?" Determined to portray Prabhu's painful story of agony and revolution in the form of a story, I returned home.

❑

The Top Ten

Kottayam, a small town in the state of Kerala, is unique amidst forests towards the west of the Western Ghat mountains. I have been staying here with my son Animesh's family for the last three years. It has been eight long years since I retired. In the first five years of my superannuation, as long as wife Shanti was alive, I had a happy life in my village. Having been married, my daughter is busy with her own family. Since my son and daughter- in-law work in IT companies, they can hardly find time to come to the village. Hence for one year after my wife's death, I cooked on my own and stayed in the village. However, after the gradual deterioration in my health, my son has brought me here to stay with him. With such a disease-prone body, it is very difficult for me to adjust with the hectic busy life of my son and daughter-in-law. But there is no other way out. The swelling in my joints has rendered my body incapable of doing anything. My son is getting me treated by the best doctors of Cuttack as well as Kottayam. Still there has been no perceptible relief. In their hectic routine life, Sunday is the only holiday for my son and daughter-in-law. So I hesitate to share the worries about my body with them frequently. Moreover, here I don't have any Odia speaking friends to share my joys and sorrows. I cannot converse with the local people in Malayalam language as I don't understand it. I can just manage to buy the grocery and vegetables with sign language. I cannot even properly express the symptoms of my disease before the doctors here as I don't know the local language. The grief and agony inside my mind always perturb me.

One day while strolling on the road in front of our house, I gathered my guts to get into the lane at the back of our house. I noticed a long queue of people in front of a hospital. I could not read the signboard properly but I could guess from the pictures on the signboard that it was an *Ayurvedic*[6] Hospital. I showed my swollen knees to one of the patients going to the hospital. I could guess from what he said in his language that this doctor could cure such diseases. With hope and courage, I decided to visit the hospital in the morning on the following day.

The next day I put all the old prescriptions in a polythene bag and started out for morning walk without informing my son and daughter- in- law. I had a spare key of the house with me. My son and daughter-in-law start out for work at 8 am in the morning and come back by seven in the evening. I decided to go back to the house only after consulting the doctor. As I had reached early, I could easily get a chair. However, by that time, nearly one hundred patients had already reached though it was very early in the morning. I heard that the doctor was a very renowned *Ayurvedic* doctor and could treat the disease completely by identifying the root causes. I silently chanted the name of Lord Jagannath and waited

---

6   *It is an ancient Indian medical system, based on ancient writings that rely on a 'natural' and holistic approach to physical and mental health. Ayurvedic medicine is one of the world's oldest medical systems and remains one of India's traditional health care systems.*

there patiently. I was wondering how I would describe the symptoms to the doctor. He won't understand my language. So, my main worry was how to convey my pain and feelings to the doctor. Only by looking at my swollen legs, he might be able to understand all that he could.

The whole area of that clinic was filled with the aroma of *ayurvedic* medicines.I could also faintly hear the sound of some treatment going on inside. Every patient was being examined for half an hour and then s/he was sent to another room for massage, physiotherapy and fomentation. It was painful for me to sit for a long time with my legs dangling down. All of a sudden "Oh Lord Jagannath, please save me" spurted out from my lips. After sometime a young man came out and asked in Malayalam who said like that. All present there pointed their fingers at me. The young man came to me straightaway and asked in Odia, "Are you from Odisha?" I was surprised. Then the young man closely looked at me with attention for some time. Then he asked, "Are you Braja Sir?" I was astonished as I could not recognize the gentleman. I said, "Yes, I am Mr Brajakishore Tripathy. I retired from Alanahat High School as the Headmaster eight years ago. Bowing down, the young man touched my feet and offered his obeisance. He continued, "Sir, are you not able to recognize me? I am 'donkey', your student, My name is Sushant Nayak. But I was popularly known as 'donkey" in the school, by the name that you had given me." I said, "My dear, I cannot see properly and my memory fails me, so I cannot remember."

The young man said, "No problem, Sir. Please get up. Let me first examine you. Sir, how have you become so weak and lean?" Then the young man took me to his own chamber. Looking around, I could conclude that the young man was none other than the doctor in the hospital. Though I heard his name, I could not remember anything about him. However, the way he brought me to his chamber in close embrace, his intimate touch calmed my restless mind to a great extent. I felt as if an angel was holding me in his arms and assuring me of my quick recovery. He made me lie on a charpoy and instructed his attendants in Malayalam to keep a few things ready and started closely examining my body. As a doctor, he asked me so many questions in Odia and listened to my answers patiently. I felt light as finally I had been able to share my pains and symptoms with the student doctor in such great detail after so many years. The attendant took me to a neighboring room. He applied and massaged the medicinal oil on every joint of my body, particularly my knees with a lot of care and sincerity. He then fomented my whole body with hot steam. He also gave me two tablets to take with the medicinal tea and then tightly wrapped a smearing of herbal paste on my knees. What a relief! The happiness was ecstatic for me. I felt as if I was enjoying heavenly bliss. The student doctor gave me some *upma*[7] and *chutney* in a plate and said, "Sir, please have this breakfast and take rest. After examining the patients I will take you to my residence. Mother will be happy to see you. We stay inside the premises of this hospital only."

Having got some rest, I could not know when I had fallen asleep so calmly and effortlessly. I woke up only when the doctor came, cuddled my head and called me. He

---

7 *Upma or Rava Upma is a classical, delightful South Indian dish. It is cooked by dry roasting semolina / sooji & then cooking it with ghee / oil, tempered onion This is savoured with sambar, chutney, powdered jaggery, powdered peanuts and sugar. It is a wholesome dish that can be cooked in minutes.*

said, "Sir, it is already 2 pm. Let's go home. I have informed mother. She is waiting there to serve us lunch. He requested me to sit in a wheel chair, pushed the chair on his own and took me to his residence at the end of the long verandah.

An elderly lady came and paid obeisance to me. She said, "Braja Sir, hope you are doing fine. I am Sushant's mother. You are not acquainted with his good name. You used to call him "Aye donkey". That may be the reason why you are not able to recall his name. I said, "Yes, I often called students by the names like donkey, stupid and urchin. That was many years ago. Now it is a crime to use such words. Now the school premises are free from any punishment. Such discipline is rare nowadays." Meanwhile, Sushant's mother served food to me and Sushant. Delicious Odia cuisine. It was more a prescribed diet than food. During lunch, Sushant told me, "Sir, black-gram, sour food items and chilies are strictly forbidden for you. The medicines won't work if you don't follow these dietary restrictions. The disease has gone chronic. You will be under my treatment for a whole month. You will have to come in the morning, have your treatment and food here and then go back home in the evening. Is it Ok for you Sir?"

There was no scope for me to say anything. But one question arose in my mind, "How did this student land up here? Why did I call him 'donkey'? He still remembers those unpleasant things even after so many years. After lunch Sushant's mother handed over a *paan*[8] to me and said, "Sir, this *paan* does not taste like the *paan* grown in

---

8 *paan, also spelled pan, is an Indian after-dinner treat that con-sists of a betel leaf filled with chopped betel nut and slaked lime. Other ingredients, including red katha paste (made from the khair tree are often added to enhance taste.*

the fields in Odisha. It is very strong."Having put the *paan* in my mouth I asked Sushant, "Dear, now tell me how you landed up here. When did you study in Alanahaat High School? I can understand that you are still unhappy and anguished as I called you 'donkey'. I am repentant of that." Dragging the chair close to me Sushant started narrating his story. His mother sat close to us.

"Sir, my mother wanted to rear me up with a lot of difficulty and dreamt of a bright future for me. My father was a watchman in the village. One day a gang of thieves tried to break inside the temple of the village Goddess. When my father protested, they hit him with an axe and he succumbed to it. By that time, I had completed Class VII from the middle English school. I had the ardent desire to study more. Mother could read my mind and did everything to support me: working in the paddy fields, boiling paddy, sewing rags and laying the cow dung cakes. Being mentally ready to bear the expenses for my studies, she took me to you. I was admitted in Class VIII. At that time, you were the Headmaster of Alanahaat High School, a popular, powerful and renowned teacher. You had a lot of clout. You had the reputation of being the most competent mathematics and science teacher. Everyone was scared of you. You were from our village. You were very much aware of our financial condition. So mother took me to you with the great hope that you would motivate me to study under your mentorship and supervision. Mother managed to provide my school fees, books, notebooks, pen, pencil with a lot of difficulty. But I was made to sit in the last row because I was poor and was not doing well in my studies. Children of well-to-do families like Prasanna, Sabyasachi, Suresh, Gouranga were allowed to sit in the front row under your direct supervision. You used to give us homework regularly which I could not work out. Other students had their parents and tutors at home to provide them academic support, explain the topics and help them do their homework. I did not have this facility at home. Even in the class I could not understand at one go whatever you taught me. Since I was sitting in the last row, often I could not hear what you said because of the intervening noise from other rows. So I used to get beaten everyday for my poor performance and then got the brand name 'donkey'. This afflicted my mind with anguish and self-pity.

One day, fed up with this kind of treatment I retorted, "Sir, please explain me these learning concepts in detail. I can do them if you can explain them to me again." You got annoyed and shouted at me, "Do you expect me to explain each one of you one by one? How can others do it? You are the son of a watchman. How do you expect to study well?" Having said this, you thrashed me black and blue. Having been physically abused and humiliated like this, I fell ill and suffered from fever for 4-5 days. Since that day I started despising the school. Mother tried to convince me but I did not go to school. Being helpless, mother wept a lot and finally reconciled to the circumstances and kept quiet. I stole 10 rupees from mother's Almirah and came to Cuttack as I didn't have any skills to look for any work. I told someone in the bus stand to inform my mother that I was going to Cuttack. I planned to inform mother after I got some work. I started working in a bicycle repair shop, since it was the only work I knew as I used to repair my bicycle on my own. While working in the bicycle repair shop, I observed one elderly man on the opposite of the road thrashing something in a stone mortar with a pestle. On other days, he used to thrash some dry things in the mortar. One day I asked him, "What do you thrash every day? He said, "I am a *Kaviraj* (an Ayruvedic doctor).I am required to prepare medicines by thrashing and grinding the natural herbs and roots. I have to identify the herbs and roots as well. Though there is a huge demand for these things in the market, I am not able to supply them in such large quantities. My son has an *ayurvedic* medicine store in Kottayam in Kerala. He often comes here to take medicines and raw herbs." I asked, "Are you looking for someone to hire to help you?" Happily he replied, "Yes, I am looking for someone to help me in identifying and collecting the medicinal roots, herbs, barks, leaves for me." I said, "Sir, I have some knowledge about medicinal plants. I am aware of the presence of many medicinal plants in the Dhartangagada   jungle near our village. I can collect them if you can help me once to identify them." The gentleman agreed. I could see that the gentleman was a wise and scholarly person. So I gave up the job in the bicycle repair shop and started helping him in his work. With my greater involvement in the work, the work became easy for me in course of time. The *Kaviraj* too earned handsomely out of this new arrangement. He started liking me and gave me handsome remuneration. I went to the village as per my convenience, gave some money to mother and bought grocery for home. Afterwards I didn't allow mother to work outside.

Gradually I learned how to prepare medicines from the elderly *Kaviraj*. He explained me the symptoms, the treatment procedures and remedies for various diseases. I became an expert in moving in the jungles like Chandaka, Barbara, Dhartangagada and identifying the plants, herbs, creepers etc. which have medicinal values. I thoroughly studied the ancient documents, scriptures, books on *Ayurveda*. The *Kaviraj* also taught me Sanskrit. I read the famous book on *Ayurveda* in Odia by Shri Laxmana Mishra with a lot of sincerity and attention. I found it very useful. I grew up with the love, care and education imparted by the *Kaviraj*. I did not understand many of the things related to *ayurveda* but he was so caring and understanding that he explained and showed them through experiments.

His elder son Bijaybabu came from Kerala after a few days. Having noticed my expertise, he brought me to Kerala with him. Since I knew the names of the plants in Odia, it became easy for me to follow him and collect the plants and herbs from the Western Ghat mountains. The medicines prepared from fresh plants, herbs and leaves proved more fruitful and effective. So the medicines sold well and earned good revenue. Some of the medicines even got patented. Bijayababu got me admitted in an *Ayurveda* school. Sanskrit was the medium of instruction there. So I did not face any difficulty. Having completed Diploma, I applied for my registration for *ayurvedic* treatment and *panchakarma*[9]. Meanwhile Bijaybabu started a factory for *ayurvedic* medicines in Thrissur. Handing over the old shop in Kottayam to me, he shifted to Thrissur with his family. The medicines manufactured in his factory are now being imported to foreign countries. I am now looking after his old shop and the house attached to it. Simultaneously I am running this hospital as well. I have also called mother from village. We mother son duo are leading a happy life by preparing medicines and serving people."

With a deep sigh, he continued, "Had you helped me a little in understanding the lessons, I could have become someone today, Sir."

---

9 *It is s a natural treatment that detoxifies and reinstates the body's inner balance and energy. It cleanses the body of un-wanted elements. It involves five (pancha) procedures (karmas).*

I looked at him with my eyes wide open. Now I recollected everything in detail one by one. Alanahaat High School had a lot of reputation from 1974 to 1979. The students of this school continuously figured in the list of the top ten students in the matriculation for four consecutive years. Hence my confidence and arrogance had magnified manifold. I was madly trying to get four to five students included in the top ten students by working day and night for the best students of the board examination. In this process I neglected the studies of others. Resultantly, the pass percentage of the school got reduced and after five years not even a single student passed in matriculation in first division." I continued, "Dear, you have said the right thing. At that time, I was really blind. Now I can see everything though my eye sight has gone weak. In the eyes of a teacher, all students should be equal. It is the responsibility of a teacher to take care of the children who are weak in their studies. It is a sin to discourage and ill-treat the weak and poor students with harsh words. I have committed that sin, dear. Though you did not figure in the list of top ten students by academic standards, you are among the best ten by the standards of humanity. You have become a healer of pain for so many people. You are returning a new lease of life to the people who are in distress and on the verge of their death." Having said this, I got up. The student doctor said, "Sir, where are you going?" I said, "Let me go home slowly. I need to sleep at home." Sushant said, "Sir, I can't allow you to do that. Now I am your teacher and you are my student. You will stay with me for a month and get treated under my care and supervision. You can go home only after you get completely cured. Sir, let me just go and send a message to your son." Having said this, the Kaviraj student Sushant got up and went out. ❑

The Dare Dreamers

It was February. Winter was about to wither away. Two years ago, at this time a sudden official tour to a rural school was fixed. The plan for constructing the new building of a primary school was being prepared under the Sarva Shikhya Abhiyan. I was deputed to this place to discuss it in a meeting of the members of the Panchayat Samiti of the village, members of the Village Committee, the teachers of the school and the guardians. Director, Odisha Primary Education Programme Authority (OPEPA), had given me the responsibility to coordinate the activities. This was my first visit to Kandhamal district. Moreover, I could not avoid the fragrance of the forests and the clarion call of the mountains. I accepted the responsibility with a lot of enthusiasm.

Starting from Bhubaneswar in a night bus, I arrived at Raikia early in the morning. Winter had waned in the coastal districts but it was still very cold in this interior part of Odisha. In this land surrounded by forests, winter morning set in a little late. The school was about 3 kms away from the bus stand. Only man-pulled rickshaws were available to travel on the rough and damaged rural roads. There were a couple of rickshaws standing in the bus stand.

Hiring one of them I started for the school. As I was a lady from outside, the rickshaw puller took the rickshaw on the narrow road with utmost care and caution. On our way to the school, we had tea in a small stall. With the fog all around, it was difficult to see one another's face but the fragrance coming from the newly bloomed mango blossoms filled the air and enthralled me. While sitting in the rickshaw with all restraint I enjoyed listening to the family story of the rickshaw puller. I felt lighter and happier in the soft fluffy fog of February.

It was only 8 O' clock when I reached the school. The official work of the school was to start at 10 am. The school was located in a rather solitary place. The rickshaw puller dropped me there and went back on the plea that someone else had reserved the rickshaw. I was clueless about where to wait for such a long time. The main gate of the school was locked. It was not possible to know whether there was someone inside or not. I thought that either the peon or the watchman would be there. I would send the message regarding my arrival through them but no one could be seen around. Having no other way out, I sat down on a big boulder in front of the school building.

Sitting alone in an unfamiliar place was very boring. As I was almost awake all night in the bus, I too felt very tired and dizzy. I could not see any water around that place so that I could wash my face. I didn't want to use the drinking water from the bottle for washing my face. At this time, I could see an old woman coming towards me with a slouching gait. However, she was a ray of hope for me. The old woman carried a half broken earthen pot filled with water mixed with mud and cow dung. When she came close to me, I could see that the tribal woman was very weak and there were deep visible wrinkles on her skin. She must be more than eighty. Her backbone had been bent outwards which forced her to stoop frequently while walking. Seeing me sitting near the school gate, the old woman was surprised. She put down the pot on the ground. Supporting her waist with her hands, she stood upright to throw a glance at me. Though I could not understand her Odia language mixed with a tribal dialect, I could understand her question and answered them mostly with signs. At first she could not understand when I said that I had come from Bhubaneswar. Then I pointed at the school and said that I had come from the city for a meeting in the school. Then she asked me in broken Odia, "Are you the Inspector?" I was happy that she was acquainted with the word 'Inspector'. Signaling me to follow her, she moved towards the gate. I wondered how the old woman would enter the school as it was closed. The hedge of grafted creepers was stretched from both sides of the gate. The old woman pushed the fence aside and made way for me. Both of us entered the school premises through the narrow passage. The old woman took me to a tube- well inside the premises. She pressed the tube well handle and asked me to wash my face, hands and legs. I felt refreshed after washing my hands and legs. The old woman spread a date-palm mat on the ground and asked me to sit on that. Then she entered one of the classrooms. I guessed that the old woman was a labour engaged to daub mud and cow-dung paste on the walls of the school. I couldn't help pitying her as she was forced to work even at that age. She went to the tube well in between to add water to the mixture in her earthen pot. The old woman had bent down a little only because of her old age but she had been able to overpower work and enslave it. Climbing up a small ladder, she could daub the four walls of a classroom with the mud and cow dung paste within an hour. She even leveled the uneven portions of the wall by throwing mud into the damaged portions. Sitting on the verandah I carefully observed the way the old woman was carrying out her work. The odour coming from the mud, the soiled hands of the old woman and the maroon red walls reminded me of the school in my own village. I went on thinking about the rural schools which had not undergone any significant changes in the last 40 years. There must be many such schools in Odisha which might be in similar deplorable conditions. Under the Sarva Shikhya Abhiyan, at least some school buildings are being constructed, no matter whether there is any improvement or not.

Having daubed the walls with the mixture of mud and cow dung, the old woman came and sat down beside me. She kept the earthen pot with the cow dung paste away from me. She thought that I might despise the unpleasant odour coming from the mud-mixed with cow dung. But I could not help my eyes moving in that direction. Perhaps the old woman did not know that I too had started my education from a mud-walled school building plastered with mud and cow dung.

There was still an hour left for the school to open. I asked the old woman if she had any other room to be daubed with mud and cow dung. Wiping out her sweaty face with one end of her dirty *saree* she said, "No, I am not going to daub the walls any more. I will daub the floor of the next room after the school time is over. Children will tread upon them and spoil them if I daub it now." I asked her about the wages she got per day. With her face down she said, "This is my own work in my own house.

What wages shall I claim for this?" I could not properly understand it. I thought that perhaps her grandchildren were reading in the school. Hence the old woman was contributing to the school on behalf of the mother-teacher association. However, I was curious to know the exact reason. When I asked, the old woman said in reply, "No dear, there is no one in my family, who would read here." I was in a dilemma. But I became more curious. If the old woman has no one in her family, why does she work so hard for the school? Why does she selflessly wipe and daub the classrooms in the school regularly? Why does she have so much of fascination for the school? I was inquisitive to know the exact reason, the story behind this act of her social service. Bringing the old woman's head close toward me, I asked, "Auntie, why do you work   so much for the school? The pale and dim eyes of the old woman welled up with tears. Wiping her tears with the end of her *saree*, she narrated her story.

My dear, the house that I daubed just now was my own thatched house. The premises of school that you see was my garden and my maize and millet fields. Bipin Bahal was my husband. He had completed Class V at that time. We earned our livelihood by working here. My husband used to teach small children in the little non-formal pre-primary school that he had started here. We were not blessed with any children of our own. I was very disheartened about it. But my husband always used to console me with the words, "Look Sevati, if you had your own children, they might have been either two or five. Now twenty children read on our verandah every day. Don't you think they are just like our own children?" I used to convince myself with my husband's words of consolation.

However, there was not any scope for higher studies for children after they completed their education from the pre-primary school. The primary school was in Kudumma village on the other side of the jungle after two villages. There were bears in the jungle. They created a lot of trouble for people. That's the reason why children could not dare to go so far across the jungle to read. My husband, accompanied by the village head, met the BDO a couple of times to start a school in the village. Permission was granted to start classes up to Class III after a lot of running around and persuasion. But we did not get any financial assistance from the government. We had sold out whatever silver ornaments that I had to meet the expenditure for running to the nearby town for this work. However, we both were happy because our efforts were going to bear fruit and a school was to be opened in our village.

One day after returning from the town my husband told me, "The school will start from tomorrow. Please remove our boxes, clothes and utensils from the house and put them on the verandah to vacate the house. Then paint the house with maroon colour. A government officer will come tomorrow to oversee the opening of the school here. Let me prepare the list of children who would be reading in this school." He was so happy that I could not dare to speak anything, lest he should get upset. In the night, he tore apart a log of wood and prepared a chair for the class. In my house, I have carefully preserved the chair and the cane that he had prepared. When I look at the chair, I visualize him sitting on the chair with a cane in his hand and asking multiplication table to children. I feel as if everything happened yesterday only. All the events always keep on dancing before my mind's eye.

This is how the school started. We constructed two more thatched rooms with our own hands by using the trunks of palm trees. The school ran as per the convenience of children, sometimes in the morning and sometimes in the afternoon. My dear, people in this area are mainly tribal people and people from the farmer and labour communities. Hence our children are required to do many things like working in the fields, picking the *mahula*[10] flowers and crushing the lime stones. We also work in the fields on wages after the school is over. So the teaching in the school is carried out by taking all these things into account. Sometimes children also come hungry to the school to study. I must have served millet porridge to children with my own hands on many occasions.

This way the school ran for five years. Then the school was upgraded from Class III to Class V. Only me and my husband had to manage the school on our own. My husband used to run to the town time and again with the hope of getting some financial aid from the government. The government officers would make tall promises but we did not get any support. People from the village supported us in terms of kinds like rice, *mahula* and millet. This way all was going on well. One day, all of a sudden some government officers arrived here in a vehicle. They called us and said, "This school will be shifted from here. Government has decided to start a school with classes from Standard I to High School as the Missionaries have come forward to provide all primary financial assistance for the opening of the school." We felt as if a thunderstorm had struck us. Will our labour and efforts invested for ten years go waste?

---

10 One of the East Indian trees with nectar-filled flowers that are used for food and preparing an intoxicating drink

The villagers got united for this cause and protested. Finally the government officers suggested a plan. If anyone of our village could donate five hectares of land for the establishment of a school, then the school could be established here. There were many reputed farmers and *zamindars* in the meeting but none of them came forward to donate land for the school. My husband looked at me in a questioning glance and I nodded my head in an affirmative gesture. He stood up and announced in front of everyone, "I am ready to unconditionally donate my home and whatever land I have for the school." Everyone clapped in appreciation but I couldn't control my tears rolling down from my eyes, not knowing whether they were tears of sadness or happiness.

Dear, the thatched house that you see was the first room to be constructed. Classes from I to VI are run from our thatched house and the higher classes are conducted in the concrete building. My husband had not passed matriculation. So he worked there as a peon. But he did not have any ill-feelings about it. He did everything with a lot of interest and enthusiasm. He also used to teach mathematics and literature to the children up to Class III. In course of time, the school got upgraded to a government school and new teachers were appointed. The school ran in this thatched house during the day and we spent our nights here during the night. However, after a few years, a strict Headmaster came and did not allow us to stay in the school premises. He said that the land and the plot did not belong to us. Where could we go? We built a thatched mud house with palm trunks near the river and started living there. My husband did not mind anything. He used to say, "Sevati, what are we going to do with our land and plot? There is no one after us to enjoy all these things. It is a matter of great fortune that a school has come up on our land during our life time. The Almighty has not blessed us with any children but we can see hundreds of children playing in our house and garden every day."He forgot all the worries of life and was thrilled when he threw a glance at the school. But God's desires and designs were different. After two years, malaria broke out in this area and it badly affected the people. My husband suffered from malaria for nearly a year and finally succumbed to it. Where could I go? The school has kept me alive. I spend my life watching the school. I earn my livelihood by selling pea nuts, ground nuts and puffed rice to the children during recess.

Having said this, the old woman took some respite. She asked me, "Why have you come to the school? I gladly replied, "Aunt, new rooms and buildings will be constructed in your school. These old houses would be demolished. New concrete houses with new designs and good facilities like playground, separate toilets for boys and girls shall be constructed. All the rooms will be cemented. So you won't have to work hard anymore and daub the houses with so much of difficulty."

But the old woman was taken aback after listening to me. There was sudden spark in her lusterless eyes. With her eyes wide open she asked me, "What do you say? Are you really going to demolish all these rooms?"

I was perturbed a little. I was under the impression that the old woman would be happy to know about the proposal of the new building of the school being constructed.

What do I see now? The old woman hugged me and loudly burst into tears, inconsolably. She said, "My dear, do whatever you like but please for god's sake don't demolish these two thatched rooms. What would I daub and paint, if you demolish these thatched mud-walled rooms? I should be able to daub the mud walls of the school as long as I am alive and my limbs are active. If I don't get that opportunity, why should I live this life?" The old woman said all these things in one breath. She became emotional and lost control over herself.

After listening to her, I too became speechless for some time. Hats off to this poor old tribal lady! She does not have anyone to call her own but the whole world belongs to her. She has reared up the school just like her children. She has bestowed her motherly affection upon the school. She told me that the children used to call her grandmother Sevati. She has not been fortunate to be a mother but she has been successful to be the mother of a mother. After some silence I held the old woman's hand in my hands and tried to convince her that I would try my best to save the two old thatched rooms from being demolished.

Wiping out her tears, the old woman went out of the premises of the school building in a stooping gait and gradually disappeared in a distance.

The routine work in the school started at 10 am. The Headmaster was a little embarrassed to see me in the school before his arrival. He made arrangements for my breakfast. He had already given advance notice to the members of the school committee, village Sarpanch, members of the Panchayat and the guardians for the meeting to be held on that day. I suggested that he should also invite some senior and experienced people from the village. The District Education Officer arrived at around 11 am. The Headmaster took me round the school and showed me the deplorable condition of the premises and class rooms. He wanted all the rooms to be demolished and new buildings to be constructed in their place.

All matters were discussed threadbare in the meeting. The Headmaster proposed for a Teachers Common Room and Library. I said that it was not possible to construct so many rooms with the limited budget as the budget allocation for this purpose was limited. I suggested that some rooms would be newly constructed and some old rooms would be repaired. Moreover, if all the old rooms were demolished simultaneously, how would the school run? It would require a lot of money and time to lay the foundation and build a completely new building. Moreover, if some new rooms could be constructed with the government money, it would be convenient for the school. Two rooms were now required to store the construction materials, cement etc. So after a lot of discussion and deliberation it was decided that the main building would be left untouched and six new rooms towards the east of the boundary wall would be constructed. The money allocated for two other rooms would be used for the repair of the old classrooms. I informed them that since primary education included classes until VIII, grant was provided for the construction of maximum of eight classrooms under Sarva Shikhya Abhiyan.

I asked the old and experienced villagers about the origin and establishment of the school. They all reiterated the story that the old woman had narrated to me. In the meeting, I expressed my discontentment over nothing done to preserve the memory of the person who sacrificed everything for the establishment of the school. Addressing 'Bipin' as Bipin Babu I suggested that his old two thatched rooms should be left untouched and should be continued as the thatched rooms. I hinted that there were good number of palm trees and bamboo bushes inside the premises which could be used for the repair and maintenance of the thatched rooms. In this context, I referred to Mahatma Gandhi who insisted on the use of the construction materials available within 5 kilometers in the radius for the construction of an eco-friendly house. He also said that just like cultivating land for food, there should be cultivation of materials required for construction of houses. The quantity of iron, cement, lime available in this world is limited. But things which are available in nature like wood, bamboo, earth, palm leaves, date-palm leaves are produced and reproduced by nature time and again. Hence these materials should be cultivated for the construction of houses. I also gave the example of how the mud-walled houses decorated with Alpana art work are considered examples of culture and heritage in the cities. I proposed that after the construction of the new building, a gate would be constructed at the entrance of the building. I encouraged the villagers to propose to name the school after Bipin Babu. Moreover, I proposed to retain the original two thatched rooms in their original forms and run the primary classes in these rooms. At the end of meeting, I too showed interest to name the library in the name of Bipin Babu's wife. The villagers unanimously supported my proposals. At the end of the meeting, the Headmaster got the signature and consent of all the members on the proposals and handed them over to me. Me and the District Education Officer approved all these proposals. A copy of the letter was kept in the school for record and I retained the other copy to be submitted to OPEPA.

All the official work came to an end at 5 pm. The District Education Officer in the company of the Headmaster and two other teachers came to see me off at the bus stand. I was to return by bus at 9 pm. They all returned after the bus left the bus stand. Sitting in the bus, I recollected all that had happened during the day. I thought that I had made a tour of the life history of Bipin and Sevati, the Dare Dreamers, in the twelve hours I spent there. My grandfather's words resonated in my mind intermittently, "Only a poor and downtrodden fakir or a powerful aristocrat can establish a school."

❑

Futile Aspirations

The school environment was abuzz with a subdued rumour and mild excitement. Teachers divided in groups were also busy in discussion and critical discourses. Lady teachers in the Staff Common Room were also equally engrossed in gossip in whispers. The Headmistress of the Primary School in the nearby village had been suspended for a scam involving submission of false bills related to the supply of eggs at the midday meals. The vigilance people had caught her red-handed while taking a bribe of Rs 20,000/- from the Self-Help Group for passing a false bill for eggs. On the recommendation of the Block Education Officer, she had been suspended with immediate effect by the District Collector. Since I heard the news, my soul had been torn apart with anger, anguish and discontentment. I had the impression that women are mostly honest and upkeep their dignity. But such a downfall in a Headmistress is unbelievable! Today I was neither able to teach children with attention nor participate in the discussion of teachers. As soon as the bell for the last period rang, I rushed home straightaway from the classroom without informing anyone in the staff common room.

When I reached home, I saw my wife Suneeta feeding

our small child in her arms, moving around the house. Seeing me she said, "Look, I have prepared egg omelette today but he is not eating. He is throwing out everything. I got annoyed suddenly. I shouted back at her, "If he does not eat, let it be. Is it necessary that you feed him only egg, nothing else? Let him eat whatever he wants."

Seeing me annoyed, Suneeta was a little scared. She had rarely seen me in that mood. I went to the washroom, refreshed myself and laid down myself on the cot for rest. After some time, Suneeta came to me with a *paratha*[11] and a cup of tea. She asked, "Are you not feeling okay?" I said in reply, "No, I have severe headache. I feel feverish." Then I had the *paratha* and tea. Suneeta applied some balm on my forehead. I said, "Please switch off the light and leave me alone. I want to sleep for some time."

The room turned dark after Suneeta switched off the lights. But the fire of emptiness of childhood ignited the anguish accumulated in my mind. I could not sleep though I tried my best. My mind spontaneously went down the memory lane to the Serdunga village, a tribal village of Semiliguda. I was born in a very poor tribal family in this village. My parents managed our family with great difficulty with the paltry income that they got from crushing lime stones. The village was surrounded by hilly lands and dense forest full of tigers, bears and other wild animals. So farming was not possible there. Moreover, rearing domestic animals was also not possible for the fear of leopards, wolves and bears. So life was very difficult in this village. We brother and sister duo also often worked

---

11 Parathas are flat breads prepared with whole wheat flour, salt, water, ghee or oil. There are served with curd, pickle or different curries. This is a staple breakfast in the Indian Sub-Continent

in the gardens, maize and millet fields of others. But I was very much interested in going to school. Noticing me writing the Odia alphabets on a corn husk, a teacher from the village school got me admitted in the village school. My father was initially reluctant but observing my interest in studies he could not decline the proposal. The teacher could convince my father that if I went to the school, I would at least get good food during the midday meals everyday and become healthy. My parents also thought in the same line. At least the child would be able to have fresh lunch every day. Gradually I got highly inclined to the school. I got new books. In my absence, my sister had to take care of the house, the gardens and open fields around the house singlehandedly. Every day, after my return from the school in the afternoon, she would ask me about the menu at the midday meal and smell my hands. We were given eggs on Wednesdays and Fridays. On these days I ate my food only with lentil and with the permission of the cook I brought the boiled egg in my pocket for Nirvani, who eagerly waited for my arrival. She became very happy when she saw the egg. I was very happy to see her eating the egg so cheerfully.

One day my classmate Mangala noticed me taking the egg from the cook and putting it into my pocket. While serving food during the midday meals, the cook served me one more egg by mistake. Mangala immediately stood up, called the Headmaster and alleged that I had stolen one egg. My pocket was searched and the boiled egg was found there. Mangala told a lie that I used to steal one egg everyday and took it in my pocket to my home. All the teachers trusted what he said and scolded me a lot. I wept out of humiliation. My face had turned red in abuse and humiliation. When I reached home, Nirvani searched for the egg in my pockets as usual. I pushed her away in anger. She fell down and cried a lot. She said, "You have eaten the egg yourself." I said, "Yes, I have eaten the egg. And henceforth I cannot bring any egg for you." Nirvani wept for a long time that day. I was in Class III at that time but I had understood the value of education. I had also clearly understood the benefits and opportunities available under the government schemes. After a few days I convinced my sister Nirvani, "Come with me to school every day. You will get rice and *dalma*[12] by lunchtime everyday and get eggs twice a week." Initially she did not at all agree to my proposal. She was scared of the discipline in the school, books and studies and above all the teachers. But after continuous persuasion for a few days, she finally agreed for the sake of eggs meal at school. My parents also agreed. They thought, "The girl is moving lonely here and there. She also goes to the jungle alone. She might meet with some mishap some day and be a target of the animals. At least she will stay protected in the school environment." With everyone's consent, Nirvani finally got admitted in Class I. She was very smart and intelligent. She was very happy in the company of her friends. In a month's time, she took care of her health and hygiene and looked fair and beautiful. She also took interest in her studies. Sometimes I too helped her in her studies.

After Class VIII I came to Semiliguda Ashram School for my studies. After three years, Nirvani too got admitted in the same school. The new school was more comfortable in every respect. There were separate hostels in the school

---

12 *Dalma is an Odia delicacy prepared by using toor (arhar) dal(lentils), and an assortment of vegetables typically raw banana, eggplant, green papaya and pumpkins.*

premises for boys and girls. Hence there was no tension of coming to and going back from the school every day. Moreover, there was advantage of timely sleeping, studying, playing and eating as per schedule. Both of us continued our studies there with a lot of sincerity and success. Nirvani came out first among so many students, even adjusted herself to the new location within a short span of time. She was a topper in every activity of the school like sports, games, music, elocutions etc. It was a pride for me to be identified as the brother of Nirvani.

I passed matriculation in first division. Acting upon the advice of my teachers, I went for D.El.Ed. training to start my teaching career early. At that time our parents were not keeping well in the village. They were not able to earn as daily wagers. So I badly needed a job. Nirvani too followed suit. She too came out first in the matriculation examination and went for CT training, though we wanted to educate her in a college. We could not afford to send her to college as I was still unemployed. Hence both of us opted for D.El. Ed. training to avail an early job opportunity. Subsequently we got appointed as Primary Teachers by Government of Odisha in the schools of two neighbouring panchayats under Koraput educational district. Meanwhile Nirvani got State Government Award as the best teacher. She was very daring and hard-working. She was a leader in every activity in the school. As a tribal lady teacher, she had been able to take advantage of all the government schemes and facilities. That's the reason why she got promotion much faster than me. She became a Headmistress of her school much before me. She is highly ambitious. She wishes to rise higher in the ladder of success in life, move to different countries, buy new houses and ride cars.

Meanwhile, she has also got married to a suitable guy. Her husband is a clerk in the local Tehsil office. Now she is blessed with a daughter. She is complete in all respects. But what has she done today? What she has done today is simply unbelievable. How could she forget her past, her roots while doing such an evil deed? Can a woman degrade herself so low just for the sake of money? We both have happily overcome so many physical and financial problems, wants and deprivations. Today just for the sake of Rs 20,000 Nirvani has put all our dignity as teachers at stake. Headmistress Smt Nirvani Tudu has been caught red handed by the vigilance team and has been suspended. I am reluctant to take the name of the same sister of whom I was so proud one day. Throughout the day I kept myself away from all. I was afraid that I might violently retaliate if someone said anything against Nirvani. My eyes got blurred with tears. Had it been some other issue, I would have rushed to her as her elder brother. But I don't need her anymore today. There was a time when she searched for egg in her brother's pocket to eat it. But today she is involved in a scandal related to eggs. I thought of going to her and reminding her of all those things of the past. But now she has moved so far off that she has forgotten her family dignity. She cannot even visualize the sacrifice of her brother and parents in bringing her up.

My headache increased in its intensity. I could not even dare to share this news of scandal with my wife Suneeta. There is a saying that, "A boil on the buttock cannot be seen or shown either." So I tried to sleep with my face sunk in the pillow.

❑

An Honest Confession

It was the 30th of November 1980. Having completed 32 years of teaching career, I retired as the Headmaster of Tarikunda High School today. Some hours ago, my students had organized my Farewell Meeting on the verandah. Teachers and students were full of appreciation for my successful teaching career and my commitment as a teacher. I felt very uncomfortable when I heard such words of appreciation. But usually in the farewell meetings one notices such words of appreciation aplenty. I too spoke my part but kept it short. My eyes were getting flooded with tears. Thinking about my retired life ahead, I felt my throat getting choked. During my period of service here, teachers and students were worried when I took leave even for a day but henceforth they will not look for me anymore. When I was about to start for home after the meeting was over, Amiya Sir said, "Let's go sir. I will carry the bouquet and gifts to your home."

By the time we reached home, the sun was about to sink in the horizon. I sat on verandah after getting myself refreshed. My grandchildren first of all opened the gift bag with a lot of curiosity. My grandson said, "Grandpa, there are 24 pens and 9 diaries." My granddaughter said,

"Grandpa, there are six story books and two books of the Geeta. I slightly overheard what they said but did not say anything in reply. I was downcast and was not very happy. I asked my wife for a cup of tea. After having tea, for reasons not known to me, I went out with a shawl over my shoulders and a torch in my hand. My wife asked, "Where are you going again? Cold has already set in. "I said, "No, just like this. Let me come from the evening walk."

I could not know when I reached the large gate of the school. Our peon Kanduri had not locked the gate yet. He came running when he heard the sound of the gate opening. He was a little perplexed to see me there at the gate at that time. He asked, "Sir, have you left something behind? I said in reply, "No, Kanduri. No I have not left any physical thing but I have left behind some specific memories here. I have come here to gather them. He said, "Sir, Shall I open your room?"

"No, not at all. Now I don't have any right over that room and that chair. I lost my right over them after 5 pm. Get me a coconut-leaf mat so that we both can sit on the verandah for some time. We will discuss a couple of things. I have never discussed with you with an open mind as a friend. Today I am not your 'Head Sir'. So let us revisit some memorable moments from our experience. Kanduri, you have been the live witness to many stories in my teaching career. Henceforth we are just friends. As you were the only peon in the school, I had to confide in you in many confidential matters. The greatest quality with you is that you never disclose any confidential information related to the critical situations I faced while discharging my administrative responsibilities as the Headmaster. Having been blessed with a colleague like you I have been able to safeguard and uphold the dignity of the school in the teeth of many critical situations."

During the course of our conversation, Kanduri got me some black tea. I felt a little comfortable after having tea. I asked him, "Kanduri, you must not have forgotten the incident during the matriculation examination of 1976. It is only because of your integrity and loyalty towards me that no one other than we two is aware of this incident. This has remained a silent secret till date. Kanduri said, "Yes Sir, I clearly remember everything about the incident and very often these moments dance before my mind's eye." I said, "You know that my elder son fell into bad company and did not study well. I tried to bring him round. I shifted him from this school to Jaishola School but it was of no use. As both the schools were on the national highway, he always spent his time in the company of his friends in the market near the highway and turned into a hooligan in course of time. He did not even hesitate to run after my life and ruin my professional career."

Now Kanduri asked, "Sir, till date I have not been able to find out how you could get advance information regarding the theft of matriculation question papers. A couple of times I thought of asking you but could never dare to do so. I replied with a smile, "Let me narrate the whole story. One day before the mathematics examination, I got the roll numbers of all the examinees written on the desks of Class X and went home at around 5 pm on my bicycle. This centre had been identified as the Examination Centre of three nearby schools. During those days a vehicle from the bank used to hand over the question papers to the Centre Superintendents one day in advance. I had kept the question papers in Almirah No 7, a Godrej one, in the room of the Headmaster. Hence I was under the pressure of a great responsibility. When I had moved a little far on my way back home, I heard someone calling me from the back, 'Sir'. When I looked back, I saw my favourite student Kshirod coming towards me speedily on his bicycle and was trying to tell me something. I stopped there. Coming close to me he said, "Sir, I do not have enough time to tell you everything in detail. There is an urgent piece of news in this slip of paper. After reaching home, please read the contents and tear off the paper. There could be threat to my life if they come to know about it."

Reaching home I refreshed myself and came to my room. I read the letter carefully.

"*Sir, today at around 3 to 4 pm, a group of non-student hooligans were sitting in the grove close to the compound at the back of the school and they were planning to steal tomorrow's question paper in the night today. As I was urinating at a distance, I could silently overhear what they were discussing. Your son was also there in that group. He has got a duplicate of the key of the lock of your room. They will enter the premises of the school between 2.30 to 3 am. Sir, please do not disclose my name anywhere. They may kill me.*"

Yours sincerely

Kshirod

"I felt as if a thunderstorm had struck me. Examinations of two papers would be cancelled. Everyone would consider me guilty and would cast aspersions. I was sure that my suspension was inevitable. This school, me and my family would be blamed for this heinous work. If the question paper is leaked, it would be a topic of discussion all over the state. The news would be published in the newspapers.

I lost all sensible thoughts for some time. Then I gathered my guts. I asked my wife Mandira to prepare dinner early. I told her that I had to eat early and sleep early so that I could I could get up early in the morning to go early for the examinations. I had my dinner before 9 pm and had half an hour rest in my bed. Then I closed the door from inside. The room adjacent to my room was the granary and the doors of the granary opened towards the paddy thrashing yard. So I left home silently with a torch in my hand through the paddy thrashing yard and I reached the school on foot.

At first I thought of changing the lock on the door of the Headmaster. But the boys were hooligans and it would not be difficult for them to break open the door. The incident would be known to all within no time. As it involves confidential matters, a case might be lodged against me. So I secretly shared my ideas with you. Then we both came to the Headmaster's chamber. I cautioned you not to switch on any of the lights. The school was in the main market and it could catch anyone's attention. At first I took out all the question papers for the next day, put them in a gunny bag and handed it over to you. I asked you to hide it in the heap of fire woods in the attic. Then I continued my work in torch light. I had few packets of previous year's board question papers with me in my official Almirah. The old question packets had to be prepared exactly in the same way as current year's packets and put in the same place so that the miscreants mistake them as current year question papers. Putting ten question papers in the maroon red packets I wrote Mathematics, High School Certificate Examination 1976 and MIL, High School Certificate Examination 1976. I too sealed them with wax. There were two sittings on that day. It took me two hours to do this work secretly, silently and faultlessly. It was 1 am when everything was completed.

Then I locked the Almirah, locked the room and came to you in the darkness of the night. You know the rest of it."

Then Kanduri started, "Yes, Sir. I get goose bumps when I recollect how like a log of wood I leaned against the heap of firewood and spent each of the moments, in spite of the mosquito bite." After a few minutes' silence, he again continued.

"Sir, the clock struck 2 am. Then it moved on to 2.30. Just at 2.45 am we could hear some thudding sound. As they had the duplicate key, it was easy for them to open the room. Then they opened the only Godrej Almirah in your room. Your son was very much aware that you kept the question papers in the Godrej only. So they opened the Almirah with the duplicate key and took away the two sets of question papers of Mathematics and MIL.

It did not take them much time to do all this. At around 3.30 amthey all disappeared through the screw-pine (*kewada*) bushes at the back of the school. You signaled me to wait for one more hour. You apprehended that they might be annoyed to see the old question papers and might come back again. But you felt comfortable when they did not turn up until 4.30 am. As it was the summer season, the dawn was not very far and the sky had become clear. We were slightly relaxed when we saw the white smoke coming from the ovens of the tea stalls and the small crowd gathering in the market at that time. Then picking up the bag with the question papers from the heap of firewood, we both went to your chamber again. You put the questions in their original places and locked the Godrej. Then you locked the main door. I got a cup of hot tea for you from the stall in the market. You looked very weak and distressed. Having got some strength after taking tea, you walked back home.

I picked up where he ended. "Yes, Kanduri. I went through the paddy thrashing yard in the twilight, entered my room and lay in my bed for some time to stretch out and straighten my limbs. Then I attended to my daily chore at home and reached school at 9 am. There were 20 invigilators for ten examination rooms. They all arrived at 10 am. I handed over the keys to Kishore Babu, the senior-most teacher to open the Almirah and take out the question papers. Kishore Babu took out the question papers, counted them as per requirement in the individual rooms and handed them over to the invigilators of the respective rooms. I cannot describe how happy and relaxed I felt at that time. When all the invigilators had left for their respective Examination Halls, I held the picture of Lord Jagannath on Godrej Almirah No 7 close to my bosom and paid my obeisance. The Almighty had saved my dignity.

Meanwhile I called for my colleague Bidhan Babu, whose brother was posted as the SI in the Jagatsinghpur Police Station. I told him that while coming to school I heard some hooligans making plans to create some mischief. I handed over an application to him and asked him to request his brother to depute an armed police team at the Examination Centre. From that day onward one armed constable and one home-guard were deployed in the school in the night to guard the question papers.

I did not see my elder son for a month since that incident. No one at home could get any hint about this incident. In the subsequent district level meeting that year I proposed before the District Level Education Committee that the question papers should be handed over to the examination centers by 10 am everyday on the days of examinations. All the headmasters endorsed my proposal and from the next year onwards, the practice of sending question papers on the day of examinations through a vehicle from the bank started.

While ruminating over the incident, we could not know when it had struck 10 pm. Having covered myself properly with the shawl I saluted the school and said, "My dear School, Giver of Knowledge, I might have done some injustice to you unknowingly during my tenure here. Please forgive me."Kanduri accompanied me up to some distance and then I moved on towards my residence.

❑

From Zero to Hundred

It was the day for the mathematics paper of the half-yearly examination of Class IX. Ashutosh came out of the Examination Hall with a heavy heart. He had attempted all the questions but was not sure whether he had got any of them right. Mathematics had never been his cup of tea but he had been able to manage to get average marks until Class VIII. On the persuasion of his friends, he had opted for mathematics optional in Class IX but started stumbling right from the beginning. When the teachers explained the sums in the class, he seemed to understand everything but when he tried to solve them at home, he could not work out a single problem in mathematics. When he wanted to change the optional, the clerk in charge of admissions told that the period for change of optional subjects   had been over. So he had no other option but to pursue optional mathematics along with other subjects. He could not dare to share it with his parents as he had himself chosen the subject.

Since childhood Ashutosh had made it a point not to discuss the questions after the examinations were over. So he kept the question paper in a folder which contained all the old question papers so that no one could catch hold of it and ask him about his performance in the individual questions. When his father asked him about his performance in the examination, he gave an ambiguous reply. He simply told him that it was better than before. As his father was used to his low scores in mathematics earlier, he was not very much worried about his reply. For him a better performance meant a better score and some more marks but not up to his satisfaction. His mother being educated up to the primary level, did not bother much about his scores though she took utmost care of his studies. Ashutosh too dodged questions of his friends about his performance in the mathematics optional paper. He could avoid the pressure of the situation for the time being but in his heart of hearts he knew that that he had not fared well and predicted something untoward in store for him.

As per convention, the answer scripts of different subjects in the quarterly and half-yearly examinations were given to the respective students for checking on their own and finding out if any answers had been left out unevaluated or there were some errors in regard to the totaling of marks. The answer scripts of all the papers except mathematics were distributed in the class by the teachers one after another. Ashutosh had performed well in all the papers and had scored more than 70% in all of them. Optional mathematics was the last paper to be given. When the mathematics teacher entered the classroom with the answer scripts, his heart beat and palpitation started increasing manifold. He could not look straight at the teacher. With his face down he waited for his turn. The teacher read out the marks of the students before he handed over the answer scripts to the individual students. He could notice the beaming smile on the faces of the students who had fared well in that paper. When the teacher called his name, he started trembling and sweating profusely. When he announced Ashutosh's marks, he felt as if the ground was slipping underneath his feet. It was 'Zero'. There was pin drop silence in the whole class. Many of his classmates could not believe the marks that he had been awarded. He wanted to cry aloud and yell at the teacher and the class that he was not a donkey, and he did not deserve a 'zero' in any case. With the answer script in his hands, he silently came back to his seat and closely examined the answer script. He went through the answers one by one. He could not believe what he saw with his own eyes. He had left all the answers incomplete and had not solved any one of them completely. As the teacher was very strict, he had not given any 'step' marks or 'grace' marks to make him happy. He just advised him to work hard and be careful next time.

All through the day, he could not focus on his studies. He avoided talking with anybody. He just visualized the face of his father, mother and other family members after hearing his marks in that paper. When the last bell rang, he left his seat quietly and moved towards home alone. Usually, he left the school in the company of his friends. But that day he felt so disheartened and disappointed that he did not feel like mixing with anyone. Reaching home, he threw his school bag in a corner and sat silently near the window. His mother was the first to notice that there was something wrong with him. When she asked him about it, he just pointed at the answer script. Though she didn't understand anything about optional mathematics, she could clearly see the big 'zero' on the top of the answer script in red. She could clearly visualize what kind of havoc that this 'zero' was going to bring about during the next few hours. As Ashutosh's father was not at home, Ashutosh did not have to face the music right at that time but he kept himself mentally ready for the explosive situation. He kept the answer script in such a place that his father's attention could catch hold of it immediately as soon as he entered his room.

His father came back from the market at around 7 pm. When he asked about Ashutosh, his mother told him that he was not feeling well and was taking rest in his room. Entering Ashutosh's room, his father saw the answer script lying on his table and the big 'zero' in deep red was sternly gazing at him. He picked up the answer script, went through the answers one after another and then put it back on the table. To the great surprise of everyone at home, Ashutosh's father did not say a single word about it. He looked at Ashutosh in a questioning manner and then moved towards the other room with heavy steps. Ashutosh was scared that his father would come back with a stick and would start thrashing him black and blue but nothing of this sort happened. There was a deafening silence everywhere. His sisters did not dare to either come to him or ask his father why he was silent. His mother could guess that something very serious was going on in his father's mind. As guessed, Ashutosh's father came to her and told her that it was because of his irresponsibility and oversight that such a thing had happened. When Ashutosh was not doing well in this subject in the class examinations and unit tests, he should have taken proper care of his studies, particularly mathematics. Moreover, he could see that Ashutosh had tried to attempt all the questions sincerely but had not been able to complete them properly due to lack of practice and guidance. Since he too was not good at mathematics, he decided to look for a good mathematics teacher who could provide proper guidance to Ashutosh in that subject.

After consultation with the teachers of the school, Ashutosh's father got the information that Mr Gourahari Dash was the best teacher who could help Ashutosh in this subject. He went to the residence of Shri Dash and told him everything about Ashutosh and his talent. He pleaded him to guide him in both optional and compulsory mathematics. Gourahari Sir said that Ashutosh could join the batch at 6 am in the morning but cautioned that Ashutosh had to be very serious and sincere about the work given by him on a day-to-day basis. On behalf of Ashutosh, his father committed that Ashutosh would do his best to live up to his expectations.

Ashutosh started going to Dash Sir from the next day. On the very first day, Ashutosh seemed to have fallen in love with Shri Dash. His friendly behaviour, accessibility, command over the subject and most importantly his humorous way of teaching mathematics enraptured him and removed his fear for the subject. Looking at the answer script, Dash Sir could surmise that he knew all the fundamental concepts, formulas of mathematics but he did not know how to apply them properly. Hence he did not teach him anything. He just asked Ashutosh to work out the sums from optional mathematics one after another and guided him how to go about them. This way Ashutosh could complete the syllabus of three months in a week's time and could keep pace with the progress in the class and tuition. In the class also, he took special interest in the mathematics classes, asked questions and sought clarifications whenever he had any difficulty in understanding a concept. This change in Ashutosh was surprising for many, including the mathematics teacher in the school. Being invited by the teacher, Ashutosh now dared to go the front of the class and work out the sums on the blackboard. The mathematics teacher was happy that he had taken a right decision by not giving any 'step' or 'grace' marks to Ashutosh in the last examination. He knew that Ashutosh was a good student and only because of lack of focus, attention and adequate practice he had not been able to complete the answers.

Ashutosh went on improving by leaps and bounds. Dash Sir was extremely delighted over his spectacular progress and started gradually engaging him in teaching the students from the lower classes. Small children enjoyed learning from a young boy few years senior to them. Then Dash Sir involved him in peer teaching, teaching his classmates. Initially Ashutosh was a little scared but took it up as a challenge. He thought that working on the problems raised by his classmates would help him clarify his own concepts and enhance his mastery over the subject. Moreover, Dash Sir was always there to help him as and when needed. On the other hand, his classmates were also equally happy. They found it more convenient and comfortable to work out the sums with assistance from a friend. Though Dash Sir was very much friendly and accessible, they could not ask him every silly question that came to their mind. But with Ashutosh, everything was possible. This way bonding between Dash Sir and Ashutosh got strengthened and Ashutosh kept on improving.

The bond was so intense that Ashutosh did not want to miss a single day with Dash Sir. On one occasion he even risked his life to attend such a morning session. One Saturday evening, Ashutosh's father asked him to go to his native village on some urgent work and return the next morning. Accordingly, Ashutosh went to his village in the evening itself. As planned, he had his dinner early and went to sleep. Before going to sleep, he asked his grandmother to wake him up early in the morning as he had to attend the tuition at Dash Sir's place at 6 am. Ashutosh's grandmother woke him up soon after she got up. Having finished his daily chores, Ashutosh left his native village on his bicycle. As he did not have a wrist watch of his own and he did not want to disturb his uncles or his cousins to know the time, he could not check the time when he left his village. He had to cycle for 13 kilometers to reach Sonpur, the town where his father was working. After he had left the village, he could guess that he had started too early as he did not see anyone on the way, not even a dog. After crossing the first village, he heard some dogs barking behind him but thankfully none of them chased or attacked him. When he reached the second village, he could see one person sitting on his verandah and brushing his teeth. Ashutosh got a little scared. He was scared not because he was afraid of thieves as he did not have anything to lose. He had only one ring on his middle finger which he could take out easily and give it to the thief if he demanded for it. It was a gift from his father onthe day of his sacred thread ceremony. But he was very much scared of the ghosts. Though it was a moonlit night, there were some places where the moonlight could not penetrate through the thick branches of banyan trees. While he was rolling down on his bicycle on one of the slopes, he found the shape of a lady in white *saree* standing under a banyan tree. He trembled out of fear and swiftly cycled down the slope at the highest speed possible and continued the speed until he reached the portion of the road which looked clear in moonlight. He sweated profusely but on second thought he convinced himself that the shape could have been formed due to the moonlight peeping between the thick branches of the banyan trees on both sides. Soon he was back in his natural self but he still could not see any human being or human activity in the next village. After reaching Harishpur he rushed to the ferry ghat to board the first boat to his home town as there was deep water in the river. But there too he could not see anyone. With no hope of getting across the river, he came to his friend Bikash's house. Bikash's father was dumbfounded to see Ashutosh there in front of the door at that time. He asked Ashutosh, "Where are you coming from?" When Ashutosh said in reply that he was coming from his native village, he said, "Are you mad? Do you know the time now? It is 4.30 am. There could have been any mishap on the way. You should not have dared like this. Now there is still time for the ferry ghat to be opened. It will open at 5.30 am. Please take rest for one hour and then go home." Ashutosh was shocked to know about it but having no other way out, he took rest for one hour in his friend's house. At 5.30 am his friend Bikash saw him off at the ferry ghat. It was 5.45 am when Ashutosh reached the other side of the river. Without wasting time to visit home, he straightway rushed to Dash Sir's place and reached there 5 minutes before time. Dash Sir was both surprised and happy to see Ashutosh's sincerity but all this happened because of the fire of motivation that Dash Sir had ignited in him.

With the able guidance and mentorship of Dash Sir, Ashutosh now scored between 70-80% in mathematics in every examination but Dash Sir wanted him to stay focused and work harder so that he could deliver better. Time passed by swiftly and now Ashutosh was ready for the quarterly examination of Class X. As usual he fared well in allthe papers and his performance in the mathematics optional paper was something that Dash Sir eagerly waited for. One day before the examination, Dash Sir gave him some tips and Ashutosh sought his blessings for good performance in the examination. The next day Ashutosh felt very confident before entering the examination hall. In the Examination Hall, soon after receiving the question paper he read the questions one after another and prepared a mental map of how he would be handling each one of them. He wrote the answers with full attention and utilized the full time available for the examination. Before handing in the answer script, he carefully read the answers again, meticulously checked the calculations to ensure that nothing went wrong. After coming out, as usual, he did not discuss his performance with anyone. He was confident of scoring very good marks but he could not dare to show the question paper to Das Sir forwith the fear of discovering any wrong answer after discussion.

After fifteen days, the teachers started giving the evaluated answer scripts back to the students for crosschecking. This time optional Mathematics was the second paper to be given to the students, Social Science being the first one. He had scored85 in Social Science and was optimistic about having a similar result in optional Mathematics. When the mathematics teacher entered the class with the evaluated answer scripts, Ashutosh's heartbeat and palpitation increased again. The teacher went on calling the names of the students by the Roll Numbers and read out the marks. When his name was called, he stood up from his seat and moved towards the teacher. When the teacher announced the marks, he was again dumbfounded. It was only '1'. He could not believe it at all. His friends too did not believe it as he had remarkably improved in his performance during the last one year. He went near the teacher and stood there with a pale and grief-stricken countenance. The teacher smiled at him and said, "No dear. It is 100. Hundred out of hundred.

I said 'one' because 100/100 is one. I am proud of you." Having said this, he hugged Ashutosh and patted him on his back. Ashutosh was on cloud 9 after having heard this. Tears of happiness rolled down his cheeks. He touched his teacher's feet out of devotion and respect. With the teacher's permission he rushed to Dash Sir in the next room, touched his feet, and sought his blessings. Dash Sir lifted him up, patted on his back and said, "Ashutosh, I am proud of you. You have become a role model for our students. You have shown to everyone that with hard work, sincerity and commitment to the goal, it is possible to chase your dream and be victorious." Ashutosh said in reply, "Sir, the impossible becomes possible only when people have angels and mentors like you who can discover the hidden talent in them, nurture them and help them reach the pinnacle of success."

Ashutosh's story of success depicting his progression from zero to 100 was a hot topic for discussion in the school for quite a few days.

❑

Painted Desires

Gyanoday English Medium School is one of the leading schools of Bhubaneswar, the most popular English medium school for the middle class people. The school has gained wide acceptance among the people of Bhubaneswar, desirous of providing English medium education to their children at very affordable prices. Even the not so affluent business people, small shop owners and people from the slums send their children to this school. Besides, well-to-do families also send their children to this school to avoid the ordeal of carrying their children to school and bringing them back every day. As we lived close to the school in VSS Nagar, we should have preferred the school just like others but me and my husband differed in the choice of school when our daughter was ready to be admitted in Standard I. I had completed B.Ed. from RIE Bhubaneswar and had the opportunity of teaching in different reputed schools of Bhubaneswar as a trainee teacher under the school experience programme. Therefore it was natural on my part to dream of getting my daughter Bithika educated from one of these reputed schools. But my husband was an ASO in the Secretariat. His salary was not so lucrative that we could dare to afford schools like DAV or Sai International. As we got blessed with a daughter within two years of our marriage, I could not get the chance to seek employment anywhere. My husband Amulya told me with a smile, "Look, you have got a young student now. You can look for a job after she grows up." He found a very easy solution to the dilemma of deciding an appropriate school for Bithika. While trying to convince me he said, "Why to send her to a distant school in a bus when there is a school nearby? She is a girl child. It is our moral responsibility to provide her a safe and secure environment until she completes Class 12. The Gyanoday School is very close to our residence. You can easily walk to the school or take the scooter to drop her in the school. The school starts at 10.30 am. So there is no need to rise early in the morning. Our daughter can also comfortably read for 2-3 hours before going to school." After listening to so many logical justifications, there was hardly any scope for me for any further argument. So reconciling with my lot, I convinced myself and happily got my daughter admitted in the school.

Truly it was a great solace as well as a blessing in disguise for me. Every day just ten minutes before the school, I used to take my daughter to school on my scooter. She entered the school with her bag, water bottle and I card dangling from her neck and I waved my hands to see her off every day until she faded out in the crowd. In the same way, after the school time, she came back home happily with me. She played a little after having some snacks. A music teacher came three times in a week in the afternoon. So the time schedule of the school suited all of us. Each of us got enough personal time for everything: eating, sleeping, reading etc.

I used to check Bithika's homework in the night. I asked her to do the assignments that she could do. The rest I just explained to her and asked her to do them on her own. She showed me the homework after completion. I helped her do the homework and tried my best to make her understand the things on her own. If required I did it twice so that she could do them independently without my assistance. In the morning, I again had a glance over her homework. But I never dictated any answers to her directly. This was the method I followed to get her homework done.

One day when I was about to start the scooter for the school, Bithika told me that she had not done her English homework. I yelled at her for not telling me about that in the morning. However, having parked the scooter near the school gate, I took the notebook out of her school bag and checked the homework given for that day. She had been asked to give the synonyms of two English words. Bithika wrote the answers in the note book on the scooter itself. The two words were for Standard I: 'dark' and 'raw'. Seeing Bithika writing her answers, a couple of boys, probably her classmates, from Standard I came rushing to us and asked for the answers to two questions related to English and mathematics. There was still time for the first bell to ring. So I left Bithika inside the school premises, came back quickly to attend these students. I asked them to sit on the cement benches near the bus stand and explained the meaning of the words given as homework and helped them do their homework. The children could understand what I explained, took out their pencils and wrote down the answers. Likewise I explained the sum to both of them and encouraged them to give the answers orally. I advised them to do the sum in their notebooks during the recess for sports. I could guess that they had no one educated enough at home to help them in their studies. They did not even speak proper Odia in their homes. Hence they did not even know how to write in Odia with correct spellings.

The next day when I reached school I saw the same two boys eagerly waiting for my arrival. They expected me to help them in doing their pending homework. I could realize that they had started depending upon me very much. Hence the next day I reached the school five minutes before the scheduled time. Bithika was a little annoyed about my going to the school so early. Gradually the number of students waiting for me increased. For reasons unknown to me I felt internally happy for being able to help these students. In my heart of hearts I was a teacher. From my experience in the RIE (Regional Institute of Education), Bhubaneswar I had very much understood what happiness and excitement were involved in teaching children, what children's affection meant for me. Gradually it became a routine for me to go early and reach the school with Bithika 15 minutes before the scheduled time. Standing at the gate, I attended to the students for fifteen minutes every day. Gradually, not only the weak students but also the bright students started coming to me to seek help in doing their homework. The interest and enthusiasm of students for studies went on increasing. Children who were poor in studies started improving. Only the soul of a teacher knows what wonders a little appreciation and affection can create in a student's life.

I don't know how five years passed like this. Now Bithika was in Class V. My popularity with the students went on increasing. Now not only the classmates of Bithika but students of higher classes also came running to me with their questions when I went to the school to bring Bithika back home. I too sometimes carried things like magnets, shoe laces, springs with me to the school to use them for explaining the difficult concepts of science to the students. Sitting on my scooter, I demonstrated the activities to the students, which enhanced their love and attraction for science. Children were amazed to see the waves being created just with the shoe laces. My main aim was to create curiosity, enthusiasm and love for studies among children. Sometimes, children asked me, "Auntie, do you do tuitions at home? We would also like to join them." I shouted back at them and said, "I never do tuitions. By the way, what is the necessity of going for tuitions? You spend six hours with your teachers and your books are with you for twenty four hours. If you read the books with patience and sincerity and try to understand the contents, everything will turn out to be easy."

One day in the morning children had surrounded me in a circle. The Principal of the school was going out somewhere in his car. All of a sudden he noticed children standing around me. He stopped his car and instructed children to go inside the school premises. He also threw a glance at me. I was a little scared. I wondered how the Principal might interpret my teaching to the children.

My apprehensions came true. The next day the Principal sent for me through Bithika. I had been summoned to meet him at 11 am. I was a little scared. Bithika was a student of this school. She should not be a target for teachers because of me. I prayed the Almighty that everything should go well and there should be no harm to her.

Next day at first I left Bithika in the school and returned home. Putting on a *saree*, I dressed up like a homemaker and reached the Principal's chamber at 11 am. I could guess that a good number of teachers were already there inside his chamber and were busy in discussing something. The peon came exactly at 11.10 am and escorted me to the Principal's chamber. I paid my obeisance to everybody. The Principal asked me to take a seat. I thought he was offering me a seat as he was planning to give me a piece of his mind.

The Principal started, "You are Mrs Sasmita Jena, mother of Ms Bithika Jena in Standard V?" I said 'yes' in reply.

-You check the homework of students in front of the school gate every day early in the morning.

-Yes Sir, they keep waiting for me.

- How long have you been doing this?

-Sir, I don't exactly remember. I have been doing this since my daughter took admission in your school five years ago.

-How are you benefited from this practice?

-Sir, I have never thought of any benefit or loss in this. I just help the students do their homework. Children who could never attempt their homework earlier are trying to do so nowadays. I just provide clue to their mistakes. I encourage them to discover their mistakes and work out the problems on their own.

-What do you get from this?

-It gives me happiness and satisfaction. I have noticed that in many of the homes, children don't have educated parents. Hence they do not have any scope of getting any academic support at home.

-I hear that you too demonstrate the science activities to students from the secondary classes.

-Yes Sir, I try to create interest and enthusiasm for science in their minds through small unusable things and waste materials. I collect small things like spring, empty refill of ball point pens, shoe laces, batteries, a piece of wire, old switches, magnet and motivate them to understand the complex concepts of science with the help of these objects. One of my teachers in RIE used to explain many complex concepts of science with the help of such a collection.

-Did you teach anywhere before?

-No Sir. I completed BSc B.Ed with PCM stream from RIE Bhubaneswar.

After this the Principal took a pause. At the end of it, the class teacher of Standard V Mrs Pratima remarked, "Sir, I used to get surprised when I saw children from Standard V doing their homework so faultlessly and enthusiastically from the first class itself. Now I understand the mystery behind it."

The Principal asked me to wait outside and called for some other teachers and senior teachers. I

I sat silently outside and comforted myself with the thought, "I have expressed myself honestly and fearlessly. I have not committed any crime". I just wanted that my daughter should be safe and no one should say her anything. I was also scared that my husband Amulya would be annoyed if he comes to know about this.

However, the peon came after half an hour and took me to the Principal's chamber again. By that time some eminent persons and senior teachers had assembled there. The ambience in his chamber seemed to be a lot different. There were smiles on every face. The Principal said, "Mrs Sasmita, I have discussed your case with my colleagues. Mrs Banaja Tripathy, a senior member of our Management Committee, was one year senior to you in RIE. She knows you well. She has informed us that you were a very bright and disciplined student there. As you were a debater par excellence, you had visited Norway on a Student Exchange Programme of the Ministry of Human Resource Development for 21 days. Moreover, your intelligence was evident in the way you answered my questions so effortlessly, honestly and fearlessly. All my colleagues and members of the Management Committee are highly satisfied with your performance in the interview. As a matter of fact there is a post of science and mathematics teacher lying vacant in this school. Hence the classes of the secondary sections are getting adversely affected. We have decided to appoint you as an Assistant Teacher in the school from tomorrow. You may bring all your testimonials tomorrow for verification in our office. What do you think?"

I felt on top of the world when I got this offer. I wondered if they were playing fun with me. I promptly said, "Sir, please give me some time to think and decide. I have to discuss it with my husband as well. Moreover, if I am appointed for the secondary classes, I won't be able to help the students of primary classes. I don't want to disappoint these students." One senior teacher said, "Okay dear, you may talk with your husband and let us know about your decision. We will think about your dilemma afterwards."

Having taken permission to go out for five minutes, I came out and informed Amulya about the development. He was quite happy to know about this. In an encouraging tone he said, "Good. Now you can stay together with Bithika in the school all day. Moreover, if you are delayed in getting employment, you will find it difficult to get employment in any good school in future due to lack of experience. This is the right time. Please accept the Appointment Letter." I went back to the Principal's chamber and informed him about my decision. The Principal said, "In addition to the classes in the secondary sections, you can also teach mathematics and science in the primary section as per your convenience. Can you handle both the responsibilities?"

I replied cheerfully, "Yes, sir, of course, I can."

After a brief conversation, the Personal Secretary of the Principal handed over the Appointment Letter to me, congratulated me and said, "From tomorrow you will have to come to the school in the uniform recommended for our school teachers.

With a gentle smile, I said, "Yes, I know".

I went to the market on the scooter, purchased a pair of uniform *sarees* and came home. As usual, there was a long conversation over this matter at the dining table at dinner time. It was decided that the next morning all of us would start for the school together.

It was the first day of my career as a teacher. I finished the daily chores at home by 10 am, went to the Shiva temple nearby and offered prayers. As I had to wrap the *saree* and I was not used to do so, I knew that it could take me some time to get ready. That's why Amulya took Bithika to school. I carried my certificates, documents and lesson plans with me. That day my scooter did not stop at the gate of the school. As I was in uniform, the security guard saluted me and opened the gates. I enjoyed it thoroughly. I had asked Bithika not to share this news with any of her friends.

First of all I went to the Administrative Office and submitted all the formal documents for verification. The Head Clerk verified my certificates. Then the teacher in charge of the Secondary Section handed over the Time Table to me. She informed me that I would take two mathematics periods in the primary section every day. She said, "You can take the classes from tomorrow" but I said, "Sister, I can take the classes right from today itself." She said, "That's wonderful. You may take the first class." The first class was Science class. Some of the students of this class knew me before. They asked me a lot of questions out of curiosity and enthusiasm. Both teaching and learning were highly satiating.

The next period was in the primary section. That day students of the Primary Section had waited for me at the gate as usual but were disappointed to see Bithika with Amulya. Mrs Pramila, in charge of the Primary Section took me to Standard V. Children were taken aback to see me in uniform. When Mrs Prmaila announced "From today onwards, Mrs Sasmita Jena is your new Mathematics teacher," they were overjoyed. The whole class of 36 students came to me, shouted "Homework Auntie" and hugged me. Bithika smiled gently at a distance and enjoyed the scene. Mrs Pramila brought her to me and hugged me. My eyes welled up with tears of happiness. What a momentous and divine feeling it was! I prayed Lord Jagannath to make my career as a teacher bright and successful.

Then I asked children to go back to their seats and said, "Bring me your homework."

❑❑

Black Eagle Books

www.blackeaglebooks.org
info@blackeaglebooks.org

Black Eagle Books, an independent publisher, was founded
as a nonprofit organization in April, 2019. It is our
mission to connect and engage the Indian diaspora
and the world at large with the best of works of world
literature published on a collaborative platform, with
special emphasis on foregrounding Contemporary
Classics and New Writing.